William H

Last Stand: Surviving America's Collapse

Alamo Publishing

Alamo Publishing

ISBN: 978-0-9918881-4-6
eISBN: 978-0-9918881-5-3

Cover design: Keri Knutson

"With an EMP, almost everything powered by electricity would effectively be wiped out—not physically, but practically. Such things would simply cease to work…"

--Edwin J. Feulner Ph.D.
'FEULNER: Countering an EMP attack'
The Washington Times

"This could be the kind of catastrophe that ends civilization—and that's not an exaggeration."

--Newt Gingrich
Former Republican House speaker

"Although many in Congress and the White House tend to ignore the EMP threat, America's potential adversaries will not."

--Jenna Baker McNeill
Richard Weitz Ph.D.
'Electromagnetic Pulse (EMP)
Attack: A Preventable
Homeland Security Catastrophe'
The Heritage Foundation

For my wife. You're the rock that binds my faith.

From the Author:

Although the story you are about to read is a work of fiction, the electromagnetic pulse (EMP) it depicts and its destructive effects on our country's electrical systems are a real and present danger. Events following Hurricane Katrina gave us a glimpse into the terrifying possibilities if we suddenly lost the modern conveniences we've come to depend on. Needless to say, the consequences of such an attack would be devastating. Millions would die from starvation, lack of proper medicine, exposure and roving gangs of looters. In the end, the domino effect could lead to the collapse of the American economy and usher in a new Dark Age.

John Mack, a prepper and former soldier, struggles to save his family and community after an EMP takes out the country's electrical grid. With most electronics, communications and transportation destroyed in a matter of seconds, the nation quickly collapses into anarchy.

For John and the other residents of Willow Creek Drive, the breakdown of social order throws them back to the 1800s. As the community tries to come together, a powerful outside force appears that threatens their survival. Will John's years of military and prepping experience be enough to keep them safe?

Mixing tons of useful prepping tips into an action-packed story, *Last Stand: Surviving America's Collapse* is a must-read for any fans of survival fiction.

Chapter 1

John Mack stopped his F150 pickup at the red light and switched the cell phone to his other ear.

"What time do you expect the open house to end?" he asked his wife Diane. She was a real estate agent with Century 21. Ever since the housing market had started to bounce back, sales as well as commissions had been steadily increasing. Their family had been hit hard during the recent recession and it was a real sore point between them. Not that he had any right criticizing her choice of profession; after all, he was a general contractor. Right or wrong though, having all their financial eggs in one basket was a recipe for disaster.

"I should be home around six," Diane told him. She sounded annoyed and a little out of breath, like she was at her desk, bending over to put her heels on. Probably the same ones she said looked great, but made her soak in hot water for hours afterward.

The light turned green and John accelerated through the intersection. "Don't forget, it's your choice of movie tonight, but no romance. One more chick flick and the kids'll threaten to move out and I might join them."

"Oh, wouldn't that be nice."

The two of them laughed.

"See you at home, honey," she said. "Love you."

A few minutes later John pulled into the driveway of their house. Two stories, three bedrooms and two bathrooms. Looked a lot like most of the other houses on Willow Creek Drive, except John would be willing to bet that his was different. Last summer he'd dug down under the crawlspace in his basement and installed a concrete bunker. Most of the work had been done slowly and secretly and the job had taken months. Not even their kids, twelve-year-old Gregory or fourteen-year-old Emma, were allowed to tell any of their friends. Since then John had outfitted the bunker with an air and water filtration system and a stockpile of dried goods designed to last them about a month. John had then put up a false wall to hide the pod's location in case the house was attacked or overrun.

He'd even made bug-out bags for each member of the family, packed with the essentials they would need in case they had to flee their home.

As far as natural disasters went, the streets of Sequoyah Hills, Tennessee, a tree-lined suburb west of Knoxville, were about as safe as they came. Sure, once in a while a thin coating of snow might turn to ice come January or February, but most everyone knew to stay indoors and wait till the ice melted away.

But if John's time with the military and the wide spectrum of combat and humanitarian missions he'd run in Iraq, Rwanda and Bosnia had taught him anything, it was that you could never be too well prepared.

In the event of a short-term disaster, he could keep his family safe and sound. The bunker underneath his basement, his stockpile of supplies and the alternate bug-out location in the Appalachian Mountains north of Knoxville had each set him back several thousand dollars, but it was a price well worth paying.

Not all of John's neighbors saw things the same way. When Sequoyah Hills had been put on a water-boiling advisory last year, he was the only one who hadn't rushed to clear the grocery store shelves. Keeping your preps a secret, that was John's number one rule, but he didn't mind telling Al Thomson, his next-door neighbor, that he liked to keep a couple things on hand just in case.

"You're not one of those guys, are you?" Al had asked him back then.

"One of what?" John had replied, not entirely sure where his ageing neighbor's question was headed.

"You know. One of those people obsessed with the end of the world. Always talking about slugging out."

John's eyes narrowed in confusion. "I think you mean bugging out?"

"Yeah, that's right." Al's smile faded when he saw John wasn't laughing.

"Well, let's just say there's nothing wrong with being ready for a worst-case scenario, Al."

"No, no argument from me on that," Al had said, fumbling with the cell phone in his pocket. "Just keep in mind, whenever something bad happens, it's never more than a day or two before everything's back online, right? Police, fire department. We pay taxes for that stuff, you know."

Conversations with Al never seemed to go anywhere. Wasn't that Al was a bad guy. Quite the opposite. But John had run into similar disconnects any time people asked about his time in Iraq or Africa. Deep down, they didn't really want to hear the truth. They wanted the sanitized, fairytale version they'd watched on CNN. Bloodless combat. Precision-guided weapons.

Watching a Bradley roll off a shoddy bridge and into the Saddam Canal in Iraq, killing all on board, or the mountain of bones that lay as monuments to the

3

senseless slaughter of innocent civilians in Rwanda—
those were the ugly realities that made guys like Al
squirm. And as much as John couldn't relate to living in
ignorant bliss, before joining the army, he'd been one of
them.

That exchange with Al had taken place around this
time last year and since then the two hadn't shared more
than polite neighborly pleasantries.

Now in his driveway, John killed the engine on his
Ford F150, listening to the sound of the engine ticking
down. Next door, Al was watering his lawn and whistling.

John got out and waved. Al nodded, bobbing to the
song he had playing on the radio in his garage. The bed
of roses under his bay window were in full bloom. Al and
his wife didn't have kids. In some ways that lawn and the
greenery Al took such pains in caring for were like the
children he'd never had. That was Diane's theory at least,
and she was probably right.

"Those roses are coming along, Al."

Sheer unadulterated joy grew on Al's face. He
dropped the hose and pulled a pair of gardening shears
from his back pocket. Al cupped one of the roses and
snipped it about midway. He came and offered it to John.

"For Diane," Al said. "She'll love it."

"I couldn't."

"No, I insist." Al gave John a devilish wink and
pushed the rose into his hand. "It's important to keep the
romance strong, John. Us men have a habit of getting
complacent, if you know what I mean."

John grinned and took the rose. "You do have a
point."

"Oh, I almost forgot. Tell Diane to give Missy a call
when she gets home. The annual block party is tomorrow
and the wife wants to finalize who's bringing what."

The block party had become something of a tradition. Neighbors, new and old, would gather the first week of June in the park at the end of Willow Creek Drive. Each family was asked to bring a salad, main dish or dessert. The men organized games for the kids to play. It was a sweet way for the neighborhood to come together once a year. Build a sense of community. John had lived in suburbs outside New York City where you never knew the names of the people around you. Sequoyah Hills was different and John never stopped appreciating that fact.

"Okay, Al, I'll tell Diane to give Missy a call." John lifted the rose. "And thanks again."

Al nodded. "Don't mention it."

Chapter 2

After entering the house, John searched out a vase for the rose. The kids would be home in a few hours and the tranquility he relished during the day would evaporate like early-morning lake mist. Gregory and Emma would tell him stories about their day and all the crazy things that had happened to them. John made sure to take an active role in his children's lives. Already they were entering that challenging teenaged phase when they weren't as enthusiastic about sharing. He'd learned to talk to them about their day and ask questions in a way that didn't seem judgmental.

Greeting them after school was one of the benefits of being self-employed. He'd built his home office in the basement and soundproofed it using rockwool insulation. John worked mostly with contracts involving renovations. Sometimes that meant showing up on site to ensure the work was being done properly. It also meant a lot of paperwork and phone calls with suppliers, subcontractors and engineers.

Not long ago, he'd begun the largest project of his career. A rich homeowner in Kingston Pike had hired him to oversee a million-dollar renovation on his two-story colonial-style mansion. The truth was, the guy would probably have been better off tearing the house down and starting fresh, but John could tell in that first meeting that this wasn't about saving money. The man had made an emotional decision. He loved his home, but wanted the inside brought into the twenty-first century. Voice-controlled lighting. Touchscreens in every room. A fully integrated security system. Stress sensors in the floors designed to detect when someone was entering a room.

When the subcontractors John hired had done their work, the house would practically become a sentient being... so long as the electricity was running. John had spent considerable time trying to convince the owner to incorporate some other, lower-tech, security measures just in case inclement weather or some other unforeseen event cut the power. Of course, it wasn't a huge shock that the home owner had turned him down. After all, this was the digital age, wasn't it? Like Al had said, what could go wrong that wouldn't be fixed by city workers within forty-eight hours?

John was in the middle of faxing the latest drafts he'd received from the architect when the kids arrived home. The front door slammed shut followed by a pair of schoolbags being dropped.

Another two weeks and both Gregory and Emma would be off school for the summer, a time for family trips to the cabin John was eagerly looking forward to. Up until now Emma had been reluctant to take up shooting, even with the Walther P22 he'd bought her this past Christmas as a starter pistol. Wasn't her thing, she'd said, and he respected that. It didn't seem to matter that the skills he was preparing to teach her now might save her life someday.

He could hear the kids running around upstairs raising a ruckus and John marched up the basement steps two at a time to find out what all the fuss was about. He reached the main floor right as Gregory ran past him, followed closely by Emma.

"You better not," she was shouting. "I swear to God, you better not."

"Hey," John said sternly. "I don't wanna hear anyone swearing to God."

Both of the kids stopped, out of breath. Gregory was wearing the kind of sly smile common to little brothers around the world. It was clear he'd been teasing his sister again. Both of them were out of breath. Emma was visibly upset.

"Now does someone wanna explain what this is all about or do I send you both to your rooms?"

Emma glared at Gregory. "He's telling lies and I want him to stop."

Indignation from Gregory. "I'm not lying, Dad."

"I don't even know what you said."

"Emma has a boyfriend," Gregory spat out as fast as he could.

"That's not true," she screamed. "See, I told you he was lying."

John swallowed hard. His daughter had recently entered that age that most fathers hated. At fourteen she was starting to feel as though she was becoming a woman, but without any of the accompanying maturity or wisdom that went along with making adult decisions.

On the horizon lay young men ringing the bell and asking if they could take Emma on a date. Nowadays most of that was done in secret. Wasn't like the old days when you actually sought the parents' permission. But John tried to keep a healthy dialogue with his kids, if for no other reason than so they didn't feel they needed to hide anything from him. It set him apart from other dads, but he always felt it was better to know before things got out of hand.

8

"Well, it's normal that boys'll start to notice you," John said, feeling a bit awkward. Emma's cheeks began glowing red. Gregory buried his face in his hands and giggled.

"You're not helping, bud," John told his son. "Why don't you make yourself useful and start peeling the potatoes we're gonna have for dinner tonight."

Gregory turned to do as he was told.

"Does he have a name?" John asked Emma.

"Come on, Dad."

"OK, OK. All I'm gonna say is I trust you'll bring him over soon so I can meet him."

She nodded reluctantly. He pulled her into a hug, aware of how quickly his kids were growing up. It had been a while since they'd hit a major milestone. Losing baby teeth, learning to ride a bike. Each of those had come and gone and now here was one more reminder that time could never be slowed or turned back. If anything, it seemed to fly by at ever-increasing speeds.

Emma went up to her room to listen to music and cool down while John made his way to the garage. In addition to the bunker, he'd also invested in a black 1978 Chevy Blazer, 6.2l diesel engine, with a Westin HDX stainless-steel grille guard.

Older cars and trucks were easier to maintain and find parts for in a SHTF scenario. He liked his Blazer so much he'd even named her Betsy. Whenever a call came and John was in the garage, Diane would tell them he was out with his mistress.

But all kidding aside, Betsy was John's main bug-out vehicle (BOV) and he'd designed her for stealth and safety. These days many in the prepper community opted for the intimidation factor: camo paint jobs, armor-plating, gun ports. All that was fine and dandy, but when and if the stuff ever hit the fan, keeping a low profile would be the key to survival. That was one of the benefits of the cabin they had up in northern Tennessee. Sequestered away from any of the main highways and emergency escape routes, it had enough stored food, fuel and water to last his family close to a year. He'd also decided long ago not to leave any of his vast array of weapons there since it might encourage theft. The rest of his supplies were camouflaged well enough behind false walls and holes he'd dug around the property.

John was wiping down Betsy's hood with Turtle Wax when the front door opened. Diane was home.

He found her in the living room, removing her heels. Snatching the rose from the vase in the kitchen, he made his way over to her. "Rough day?" he asked.

She started to sigh, then giggled when she saw the rose in his hand. "You did something bad, didn't you?"

John laughed. "What do you mean?"

"Wife shows up and husband has a rose. It's on every sitcom."

"This one's for real. Compliments of Al next door."

She took the rose and smelled it, eyeing John suspiciously.

He bent down and helped her with her shoes. Diane's nose tweaked, but it wasn't the rose this time. "I smell potatoes."

John smiled. "Gregory was up to his usual tricks, so I put him to work."

"Oh, you smart man."

He was heading for the kitchen when he asked, "So, you settle on a movie for tonight?"

Diane leaned back in his favorite chair, a leather recliner, the armrests worn from years of use. "I was thinking of *The Hunger Games*."

John turned and raised an eyebrow.

"I thought you'd enjoy it. It's one of those dystopian things where a bunch of kids have to fight one another."

"Yeah, I think part of it played out in the living room a few hours ago."

Diane giggled. "The kids have already seen it, I know."

"I'm sure they have, but that wasn't why I was giving you the look."

"Oh, the look. You wanna see something else?"

"Isn't *The Hunger Games* a love story?"

Diane smiled, dimples forming in her cheeks. "That mean you and the kids are moving out?"

Later that night, after dinner and the movie, John and Diane were in their bedroom. John was removing his shirt when he glanced in the mirror and caught sight of the scars that covered his torso. That you'd carry the marks of battle with you for the rest of your life was something they never told you during enlistment. But what they really neglected to mention was that the worst wounds would be the ones you couldn't see.

Diane came up from behind and wrapped her arms around him. Her right hand caressed the lump of discolored flesh on his abdomen. That was where the flaming shrapnel from the frag had torn into him all those years ago.

"I think Emma has a boyfriend," he said, trying to convince her he wasn't thinking about old battles.

A smile grew on her face. Her eyes were twinkling. "It was bound to happen."

"She's only fourteen," John said, his heart beating a little faster. His fists clenched.

"We weren't much older."

11

The two of them had been high-school sweethearts and hadn't done much more than sneak a few kisses before they were married. But times had changed since then. John had read about kids in some of the bigger cities having sex in middle school. The thought made him sick.

"What did Emma tell you about him?"

"She denied it."

Diane slapped his shoulder playfully. "Well, there you go. And you say I get all worked up over nothing." Her hands went to his shoulders, where she began massaging a knot of hard muscle. "You can't protect them forever, John. Eventually, they'll need to fly on their own."

"Eventually," he whispered. "But not just yet."

Chapter 3

Diane dropped the kids off to school on her way to work, which was just fine with John because a ton of work lay ahead of him. He was in his basement office, sipping a cup of warm coffee, trying to calm his nerves. Two important deliveries destined for the construction site had been a no-show this morning, one a load of drywall and the other a thousand pounds of Italian marble. John would need to spend the next thirty minutes tracking down his suppliers and getting answers. Afterward, he'd hightail it to the work site to make sure everything else was going according to plan. A screwup this big could cost him the job and with their family only starting to get back on their feet after the economic meltdown, it was a loss he couldn't afford.

John dialed his marble guy first and checked the planner on his laptop at the same time to ensure he'd given everyone the correct dates.

"Sal here," the gruff voice said on the other end.

"Sal, it's John. Get Mario on the phone right now."

Sal normally liked to chitchat, but even he could tell now wasn't the time. "Uh, sure thing."

John heard Mario's name being called over the speaker system at the warehouse. A few minutes later a voice came on.

"John, you won't believe the morning we've had—"

Then the call got dropped. John began to redial and then noticed the cell phone screen.

It was blank.

But that wasn't all. His laptop was gone too and so were the lights in his basement office. The room was mostly dark except for faint light bleeding in from the doorway. If he'd closed himself in like he normally did, he would have been in pitch blackness.

You've got to be kidding me!

Hitting buttons on his cell wasn't going to do a darn thing, but John tried it anyway, the same way people tried to make elevators speed up by mashing the button over and over.

His first thought was that he'd somehow overloaded the circuit breaker.

But your laptop and cell phone are battery-powered, that little voice said.

John grabbed a Maglite he kept by his desk and went to flip the breakers anyway. It didn't take more than a second after doing so to realize the power was really out.

Running up the basement steps two at a time, John raced into the kitchen and saw that the stove and microwave were both blank. He snatched the portable phone and swore when he realized that it too was dead.

Next he went for the front door, curious to see if anyone else was having the same problem. He swung it open and when he looked outside all the air went out of his lungs. Two cars were stopped on the road right outside his house. The drivers looked confused. One of them, a man in his mid-forties, was lifting the hood of his Jeep Cherokee.

"That's just the damnedest thing," his neighbor Al exclaimed. He was fiddling fruitlessly with the knob of his radio as water ran from the hose in his hand.

14

John wondered for a moment if this was all a dream. Maybe he was still asleep in his bed. He crossed his lawn, heading for the road, feeling the grass slide between his toes as he did.

No, this is no dream. This is real.

Other cars were stalled in the distance. Most with people who were likely on their way to work. No one knew it yet, but if John was right, they wouldn't need to worry about getting to the office on time. Not for the foreseeable future.

Al was coming this way, the hose discarded carelessly on the lawn, dribbling precious water.

"Ain't this just the damnedest thing?" his gray-haired neighbor said. "What do you make of it?"

John swallowed hard. "Only one of two things can cause something like this, Al, and neither one of them is good."

Al was at a complete loss. John could tell the words 'blackout' were on the tip of his neighbor's tongue, but even that was far too mild.

"I'm all ears."

"If we're lucky it's only a solar flare, like the Carrington Event that hit in 1859, knocking out telegraph systems across Europe and North America. Some telegraph pylons burst into flames."

"Solar flare." Al sounded like a man learning a new language. "And if we're not lucky, John?"

"The only thing worse than a solar flare is an EMP."

"A what?"

"Electromagnetic pulse. A high-altitude atomic blast. If so then just about every electronic device and vehicle in the country, maybe even the continent, has just been wiped out."

"Holy cow! Are you saying I'm gonna miss *Masterpiece Theatre* tonight?"

John let out a burst of nervous laughter and so did Al. Soon both men were grasping their bellies, clenching their teeth with the pain, both of them knowing that nothing about their situation was the least bit funny.

Chapter 4

"Diane and the kids," John said once he'd regained some measure of control.

Al nodded. "I should go inside and speak with Missy. If we wait long enough, the power might come back on, don't you think, John?"

There was a heavy dollop of desperation in Al's voice.

"I might be wrong about all this, Al. Last thing I wanna do is play Chicken Little and have everyone running for the hills."

The woman and man whose stalled vehicles were stopped dead bumper to bumper waved them over.

"And if you're right?" Al asked.

"Then it won't be long before law and order begins to break down. Think about it for a second. What part of our lives isn't connected in some way to electronics? Then consider that most households have three days' worth of food. Those eighteen-wheelers on the highways you're always complaining about. Like it or not, that's how over seventy percent of the goods we need make it to grocery stores. If the cars we see are any indication, the highways have become parking lots. My advice to you, Al, is to fill your bathtub and as many buckets as you can find with water. It won't be long before even that cuts off for good."

The worry on Al's face was turning to panic as John walked back to his house. "Where are you going?"

"To get my wife and children," John replied.

The man and woman came over then.

"Excuse me, sir," she said to John. "I was wondering if you could give us a boost."

"A boost isn't gonna help you," he answered.

Other neighbors came out of their houses, looking at one another with perplexed expressions. For most of them, this was the strangest power outage they'd ever seen. But with no cell reception, no radio, television, or even internet, there wasn't any proper way of informing people what had happened.

"It's worth a try, isn't it?" the man asked. "A boost'll take less than five minutes."

John saw he'd been driving what looked like a 2011 Chrysler 300. The computer chip in his car that controlled the fuel injection and other vital operations had been fried by the high-intensity burst of electromagnetic energy. Vehicles manufactured before 1980 had fewer or no computerized components which made them an ideal choice. A diesel engine was even safer and offered the additional advantage of being compatible with certain alternative fuels like heating oil and kerosene. This was why John had opted for the 1978 diesel-powered Blazer.

"I'm sorry, but I don't want to waste your time. I'm telling you it won't do any good."

"Yeah," the man said. "Well, thanks for nothing." And he stormed off.

Once the man and woman had walked away, John went to his F150 parked in the driveway. He slid behind the wheel, inserted the key and turned it. Predictably, nothing happened. A result that didn't shock him, but he would have been foolish to not even try. He put the truck

18

into neutral and took his foot off the brake, letting gravity roll it off the driveway and onto the lawn.

He then pulled open the garage door and inspected the Blazer. This would be the real test. Betsy was not only his primary bug-out vehicle, she was his last resort. It was one thing to create several contingency plans for yourself—an older motorcycle, for example—but when you had a family and all the supplies they would need, there just wasn't enough room in his garage or his budget for another vehicle. He topped up the tank with fuel, got in and turned the key.

The engine roared to life and the sound was at once exhilarating and terrifying. With a community and probably even a city of stranded motorists, how long would it take before someone decided they wanted Betsy for themselves? Under the driver's seat was the S&W M&P .40 Pro John kept as part of his preps. There were plenty more weapons in the gun safe in his basement office, but since his objective was a lightning-fast pickup, he wasn't going to bother bringing an arsenal with him. Besides, the majority of people were currently in a state of confusion.

It would be another forty-eight hours, he predicted, before that confusion morphed first into panic, then desperation, and finally all-out violence.

All eyes in the neighborhood were squarely on John as he brought Betsy out from the garage. He jumped out and lowered the garage door. The man and woman who'd asked him for a boost earlier were speaking to one of his neighbors, Curtis. Now all three of them were looking this way, the woman's hands on her hips in disgust.

But what was John supposed to do, give lifts to everyone in the city who was stranded? He'd been honest with both of them that a boost wouldn't help them. He'd also made the quick calculation that going into details about what he suspected was an EMP attack would only lead to a string of endless questions. The truth was he didn't even know himself if that was what had happened. For all he knew, the government had been testing some kind of future weapon and something had gone terribly wrong. Course, that was stuff best left for low-budget sci-fi movies, while EMPs were a real threat to the country and its infrastructure. The other unknown at the moment was how far-reaching this was. Was Knoxville the only city out or had the entire country gone dark?

John put Betsy into gear and rolled out of his driveway, wondering how long it would be before he got his answer.

Chapter 5

Diane's Century 21 office was three miles from the house. In the old days, taking the highway might have gotten him there faster, but that was surely a parking lot and the last place John wanted to be.

He left their quiet, idyllic community of Sequoyah Hills and headed west along Lyon's Pike. These were the back roads and not nearly as congested as the highway would be.

Soon he came upon cars stopped in the middle of the road. Some of them were already abandoned. Others still had people in them. A few had ventured to nearby houses, knocking on doors and asking for help. But like the man and woman who had approached John on Willow Creek minutes before, he already knew they were beyond help.

Weaving between stalled cars, John did his best to get there fast. A man in a gray suit holding a briefcase tried to wave him to stop. And he wasn't the only one. As John had predicted, the Blazer must have seemed like a mirage in a desert of broken-down vehicles.

At the intersection of Lyon's Pike and Northshore, a group of bystanders had gathered together. No doubt many were stranded motorists commiserating with one another over the situation, wondering how they might get the help they needed. With working cell phones they could have called AAA. One more symptom of the society they lived in—the first thought in people's minds when there was an emergency was, "Who you gonna call?" They had lost all semblance of self-sufficiency.

As John approached in the Blazer, a few from the group stepped out into the road and he was forced to make a decision. Either run them over or slow down. On the plus side, Betsy's doors were locked and the pistol was under his seat. Besides, they didn't look particularly threatening. John reached down and set the S&W M&P .40 Pro on the passenger seat. The truck was high enough that they wouldn't see it just by looking in.

He rolled to a stop and lowered his window.

"Listen," a guy in khakis and a blue Best Buy shirt said in a panic. "We don't have a clue what happened, but all of our cars conked out at once."

A young girl with a blonde ponytail lifted her cell phone in the air and scrunched up her face. "Our phones are dead too."

"I know," John said. "I don't want to frighten you, but the same thing is happening in my neighborhood. Might be the whole city is affected. Maybe even more."

"Hackers," the guy from Best Buy spat. "I remember seeing a video on this a while back. Russian and Chinese hackers. They've finally done it."

"I don't think it was hackers," John told him. "They tend to target one piece of infrastructure at a time. Electricity, cell phones, but not all at once and not your cars too."

"You sure about that?" Best Buy asked.

John shook his head. "How can I be? I suggest each of you forget going to work and get stocked up on as much food and water as you can find. This outage may last awhile." It could last months or years, but now wasn't the time to freak people out.

The blonde girl was talking to herself now. "I never trusted that Onstar stuff. I'll bet you a million bucks that's what the Chinese used to hack our cars."

The conspiracy theories were starting to fly and with that John excused himself.

"Wait a minute," Best Buy called after him as John started rolling his window up. "Can you give me a lift to Kingston Pike?"

"Yeah, I need a lift too," the blonde said, waving her cell phone as though she was hailing a cab.

"I'm sorry, I can't help you. Please step back so I don't run anyone over by mistake."

"Come on, man!" Best Buy shouted. His polite veneer was already starting to crack.

John went for the pistol and stopped himself. They were scared and slipping into panic mode. He revved the engine, making it growl. "Step back, please." His military command voice came out and they did as he said.

John sped away. He'd be coming back along the same route before long and hoped the crowd would be dispersed by then.

Heading up Northshore Drive John encountered a single stalled car. It had rolled back into a ditch after the owner must have abandoned it.

A minute later, he approached the Century 21 office. The building was a red-roofed, one-story bungalow. Sharing the space was a law office and a small mortgage company. John pulled into the parking lot and stopped before the front doors. A few of Diane's real estate colleagues were milling about outside. He stuffed the S&W under his belt and pulled his shirt over it. Then he got out of the car and locked it behind him.

"Hell of a morning, John," Tom Weaver crooned, pulling hard on the cigarette clenched between his yellowed fingers. He owned the real estate branch and seemed to spend most of his time out front smoking.

"Is Diane inside?" John asked curtly.

Tom shook his head. "Don't think so. Last I saw Diane she was on her way to show a house in Cedar Bluff."

Tom rattled off the address, but what struck John most was the way they were all standing around, waiting for the power to turn back on, just as it had always done in the past.

"This may be a whole lot worse than it seems," John said. It was difficult knowing whether to come right out and scream EMP, that they should go home to their loved ones before it was too late. The average person wouldn't understand and even if they did, they were so ill-prepared for what lay ahead that it almost seemed cruel to warn them this late in the game. Even so, John drew in a deep breath and began laying out what he thought had happened. He didn't get very far before Tom cut him off.

"I know you spent time in the military, John, but I don't see how you could know such a thing."

"I didn't say I knew, Tom. I said there isn't another explanation that can account for everything that's happened this morning. The loss of power, cell phones and cars not working."

The others standing nearby were beginning to look frightened.

"I sure hope you're wrong about this, John, cause Diane's got a big property up in Oak Ridge that's supposed to go through today." Tom pulled out his pack of Marlboros, shook a fresh one loose and lit it with the dying ember of his current cigarette.

John smiled, told them God bless, hopped back in his truck and took off. This was the third time today he'd tried warning someone about what was coming and it was clear they just weren't interested in believing it. Not yet. By day two and three the grim reality would start to sink in. That was time John could use to figure out what play to make. Stay in the bunker he'd built under his garage and live off the month of supplies he'd stashed there or head north for the cabin?

He stepped on the accelerator, roaring past a man in blue jeans next to a BMW, waving his dress shirt around like a white flag. Knoxville was brimming with people crying for help all at once and there wasn't a thing the police or emergency response services could do about it. John's first order of business was to find his wife and kids and hope to God he would get there in time.

Chapter 6

The further he drove, the clearer it became that the outage wasn't limited to Sequoyah Hills. Small handfuls of stunned motorists stood along the roadside, many of them watching his Blazer rumble past as though it were a UFO. A few even chased after him, waving their hands in the air. The lost expressions on their faces reminded him of news footage from Haiti after the earthquake in 2010. Except here and now, instead of death, there was only shock. But that would change soon enough.

He reached Cedar Bluff and turned onto Eagle Brook. A minute later, he arrived at a typical suburban neighborhood, perfect for a young family. The house Diane had come to show was on the corner; red brick, yellow garage. Two cars were in the driveway and one of them was hers. Groups of neighbors were huddled outside talking to one another, many of them eyeing John as he drove in. He stopped and slid the S&W inside his front waistband. This time he wanted people to see he was armed since it might help deter them from doing anything silly.

He locked the truck and made his way to the house. The hope was that Diane was waiting with her client inside, but as he drew nearer, John's heart sank. The door was slightly ajar. That meant they'd probably exited at some point after the lights went out. He stopped next to

Diane's Ford Focus and tried the handle. It opened. Had she come out to leave and found that her car wouldn't start? Just in case, John drew his pistol and poked his head inside the house.

"Diane?"

The house was empty and the deep timbre in John's voice made an eerie echo. He let himself in, wiping his shoes on the doormat purely out of habit. John made a quick search of the house. There was no reason to head into the basement, since the lights weren't working and they wouldn't be able to see down there. It was time to look elsewhere.

As he exited the house, three men were standing near Betsy. They were talking to one another, pointing at the hood and the engine underneath. It was clear enough to John that they were wondering how his Blazer was still working when the other cars in the neighborhood were dead as a doornail. He just hoped for their sake that the men weren't hatching some foolish plan to take it from him.

They turned when they saw John approach.

"I'm looking for my wife," he told them before they had a chance to say anything. "She's five five, long dark hair, wearing a black skirt and a white blouse." The real estate sign on the lawn had Diane's picture on it. He pointed. "Any of you see her around this morning?"

One of them nodded. "Yeah, I saw her. She was with a man and a woman. They started walking up the road not long ago. Don't know where they were headed."

"Thank you," John said gratefully. "You three strike me as family men."

"We are," one of them in dress pants and a white shirt replied. "I was leaving for work when everything just shut down."

"Everything with a computer chip, that is. All you need to do is look around to see the proof of what I'm saying. I suggest each of you grab a wheelbarrow and head to the local market for supplies. Best to do it now before everything's gone. If any of you have an older car, say something built before 1980 and preferably with a diesel engine, it may still run."

"Doesn't Gary Henderson have that old MGB?"

"Yeah, he's got a couple old cars."

"Maybe you men can work something out with Gary. Barter for the use of one of his cars. Gold might work or offer a skill if you have one."

"Seems a bit premature for all of that, doesn't it?" the man in the suit said. He was probably some sort of lawyer or office worker. A skillset which would be useless in the coming months. "I mean, we'll all feel a little foolish when they get things running again."

"When *who* gets things running again?" John asked. He didn't have time to chitchat, but he was working to accomplish two goals. First, divert the men's focus from his truck to some other means of transport and second, offer them advice that might just save their lives. They didn't seem dangerous, but desperate people didn't always think straight. "Feel free to keep waiting," John said, "but whatever's going on has affected the entire city, maybe even the whole country. Please don't take this personally, but I'm gonna ask that you three gentlemen back away a few paces while I get in my truck."

They looked at him with confusion.

John dropped his hand to the pistol grip sticking out of his pants.

The men backed away. He got into Betsy and before closing the door said, "Thank you very much, gentlemen. God bless and good luck."

They nodded, still not entirely sure what had just happened.

John started the engine and left. He didn't get further than a few houses before he saw Diane talking with a group of people. They watched him approach and sudden recognition lit her eyes when she realized that it was him. She came at once, carrying her high heels as she walked across the lawn. John leaned over and unlocked the door so she could get in.

"Oh, honey, aren't you a sight for sore eyes." She leaned over and hugged him tight.

He was putting the truck in gear when she said, "Hold on. I can't just leave the Shaws."

"Who are the Shaws?"

"The young couple I was showing the house to."

"Diane, I'd like to help them, but we don't have time. We've got to get Gregory and Emma from school and then hit the grocery store before they're cleaned out."

"You think it's that serious?" The rising fear in her face was starting to show for the first time.

"If you only knew."

Diane glanced out the window at the Shaws and he knew her heart was heavy. She was a good Christian woman, always eager and willing to help anyone in need, but in a situation like this, chauffeuring people around Knoxville was only going to endanger her family. It was a dilemma John had already faced a half-dozen times since taking Betsy out of the garage. Sure, it would have been nice to help as many stranded motorists as he could. But then what would happen when things got too dangerous to risk leaving the city? The shock that had stunned and perhaps tranquilized most of the population into temporary docility wasn't going to last much longer.

They left Cedar Bluff and headed to pick up the kids at West High School. With so many high-school kids

29

running around it was going to be difficult to find Emma and Gregory, but the school's emergency protocol was to send the kids to the football field in orderly groups. Hard to imagine any evacuation going off well without the principal being able to use the intercom.

John and Diane were approaching Interstate 40 when his wife gasped. A second later he saw what she'd been looking at. Hundreds if not thousands of people up on the raised highway walking. They'd left their cars and had become a herd on a mass migration. At once it made John think of 9/11 and the thousands who'd fled Manhattan by foot across the Brooklyn Bridge.

Neither of them knew where the crowd was heading, but one of the off-ramps led to Sequoyah Hills. Surely at least a small portion of the mass would divert in search of supplies and a way home.

"We've got to hurry," John said, gripping the steering wheel and pushing the Blazer.

Chapter 7

They were driving south along Hollywood Road when they came to the accident. A pileup was probably a better way of putting it, since at least a dozen cars in both directions had collided once their engines had cut off. By now many of those involved had simply left their cars and walked away.

On one side was a narrow sidewalk next to a short stone wall. On the other was a field, but there wasn't enough room for the truck to pass by. The only other road that cut under the interstate wasn't for miles and the highway was little more than a sea of pedestrians.

"We'll need to go back to the next turnoff," Diane said, tapping the flat of her nails against the passenger window. She was deep in thought and likely feeling the same disappointment John was.

He nudged Betsy forward.

"John, you're not thinking of—"

"We don't have the luxury of going around, Diane."

She tightened her grip around the overhead grab handle. "I don't think it's safe."

Betsy's tire clearance was such that John might be able to keep his right wheels on the sidewalk while his left rolled over the stalled car blocking his path. Luckily it was a Corvette that had crashed into the opposite lane which meant the car's low hood was facing Betsy's front left tire.

"This is someone's property, John. You can't just drive over it."

"Honey, these cars aren't much more than hunks of metal now. Besides, if the insurance companies don't go completely bust then he can get it repaired."

Like nearly everyone else's, Diane's thinking was still in line with a society that had ceased to exist the minute the power went out.

John pressed the accelerator and Betsy lurched as the front tire hit the Corvette's bumper.

"I'm not sure about this, John."

In the distance, John spotted a trickle of people in business suits mixed with truck driver types and folks in casual clothing. This was the first wave descending from the raised interstate. He would have to hurry before the trickle became a flood and they blocked the street altogether.

John backed up five meters and then accelerated to build up some speed. Betsy hit the Corvette and stopped, throwing John and Diane forward in their seats. Distance wasn't what was needed. John brought Betsy right up to the Corvette's bumper and then slowly pressed the pedal. There was a groaning sound as the truck climbed and then rose up at a thirty-degree angle. Gravity kept Diane pinned to the passenger door.

"Hold on, honey, we're almost there." But the worst was about to come. The Blazer had to make it over the Corvette's roof. Now he really pushed Betsy forward, steering back and forth to keep the truck from tipping over. A moment later they were over and Betsy's back wheel touched pavement, rattling them both.

Diane gave him a nervous grin. "John, tell me you'll never do that again."

"I promise," he replied, squeezing her hand. It was true that he'd taken a chance, but a calculated one.

Up ahead was the stream of refugees from the interstate. John honked as he slowed down to cut through them. A few threw their hands in the air, as if to say, 'What about us?' John simply laid on the horn and inched forward. He'd seen similar crowds after football and hockey games let out in big cities. It didn't matter if the light was red, pedestrians would surge across the street anyway. These people were on their way home as well, but the main difference was they were getting there on foot. And judging by the looks on their faces, home was the only thing they cared about. The fear hadn't quite materialized just yet. For some it was an adventure. For others, simply an annoyance. Once they realized the nightmare was real and they weren't going to wake up from it, the real fear would settle in.

As John and Diane reached Tobler Lane, they saw West High School and the throngs of school kids out on the football field. Many of them were sitting in small groups. A few had wandered off to congregate away from the masses only to be chased down by the teachers, eager to maintain control.

John turned the wheel, avoiding a stalled car and bringing Betsy up onto school property. They were about to make one hell of an entrance, but following school policy wasn't at the top of John's list. He needed to get his kids and bring them to safety.

He drove right up to the football goal post and stopped. The S&W was still tucked into his waistband, but now he pulled his shirt down to block it from view. There was little to no chance he'd need it here. It just didn't make sense to head into a potentially dangerous situation without it. Diane came with him, locking the truck behind them.

33

The school principal Pamela Walters was already coming their way, holding a megaphone and waving at Betsy with her free hand. "I'm sorry, Mr. Mack, but you're gonna need to move your truck."

"I will, as soon as I get my son and daughter," John explained.

Mrs. Walters glanced at the crowd of kids behind her and made an expression that said, 'Good luck finding them in all this.' Children were already starting to come forward.

"I believe that something terrible has happened," he told Mrs. Walters. "There's a good chance this wasn't some freak accident."

"What do you mean?" she asked, dropping her chin slightly to get a better look at him over her spectacles.

"Everything electronic has stopped working. Cars, cell phones, computers. There may very well be a natural explanation, but no matter what the effects are going to devastate the country. A stampede like you've never seen before is descending from the off-ramp of Interstate 40. People who are confused and looking for a quick way home."

"How do you know this?"

"There's no other reasonable explanation. These kids are better off at home with their parents."

"We've already had a few come by on foot to get kids, but keeping track of them all is becoming difficult."

"Well, let me take Emma and Gregory off your hands. Having to worry about two less will surely help."

Mrs. Walters nodded. "I won't pretend to know where they are. The kids are supposed to be organized by class during an evacuation, but clearly that directive wasn't followed."

Diane approached a group of girls who were about Emma's age and asked them if they knew where she was.

34

John did the same thing to a group of boys, asking about Gregory.

John made his way through the throngs of students, who pointed to the stands, which were full of kids. Mrs. Walters followed them.

Once they arrived, Mrs. Walters raised her megaphone and called out for Gregory and Emma. She called out a second time before a boy stood up and began making his way down. It was Gregory, but there wasn't any sign of Emma.

"Can you try again?" Diane asked.

"She's over there," a girl with long dark hair said, pointing.

They all turned in the direction she had indicated. Over by the opposite goal line, two figures sat cross-legged on the grass. They were kissing.

John's heart skipped a beat.

"Gregory, run and get your sister at once," Diane said.

He did as he was told. Emma looked over and rose to her feet. So too did the young man she was with. All three of them headed over.

"Hand me that for a second, please," John said, pointing to Mrs. Walter's megaphone. She handed it over. "Young lady, I suggest you double-time it."

Reluctantly, Emma broke into a jog, along with the boy she'd been kissing minutes before. Soon, they arrived, Emma looking mortified. John hadn't intended to humiliate her in front of the entire school. The young man Emma had been kissing was thin and pink-cheeked with dark hair and fine features. John recognized him as a boy from their neighborhood.

"Does your friend have a name?" John asked.

Diane nudged him.

35

"I think we have a right to know," he told her in response.

"Brandon, Mr. Mack," the boy said, smiling weakly. "I live on the corner of Willow Creek and Pine Grove. You know my parents."

John nodded. "I met them at last year's block party." He could see the pulse in Brandon's neck and knew it wasn't from the jog. The kid was expecting to get a tongue-lashing. But right now, John had neither the time nor the inclination.

Chapter 8

A few minutes after they left West High, John pulled into the parking lot at the Publix grocery store.

"I thought we were heading home?" Diane asked him.

John turned on the radio and flipped the knob. They didn't hear a thing. It looked like not everything in the Blazer had survived the EMP.

"There's no telling how long this may last. I think we should get some extra supplies just in case."

"But we have that bunker thing in the basement with lots of food," Emma said. "And the cabin in the mountains."

"You're right," John told her. "The pod at the house has enough supplies for a month and the cabin for a year, but what if this lasts for longer than that? Besides, if you haven't noticed already, the folks around here are stunned and confused. They'll only really start to get dangerous when the food in their houses runs out."

"You still haven't told us what's going on," Gregory said. "Are we at war or something?"

John and Diane exchanged a glance. "I don't know. I'll explain more when we're back at home safe and sound."

Just as he said that, a large group of people streamed into the grocery store. Others were leaving, pushing carts out into the parking lot. Many kept on going, probably intent on pushing those carts all the way home.

"You three stay here and keep the doors locked," John told them. "If anything bad happens, head straight home. I'll meet you there."

He hopped out of the truck and headed for the Publix. As a matter of habit, John always kept two hundred dollars in cash in his wallet, so he'd have enough to cover what he was about to buy. Water was high on his list, as well as canned goods. They needed things that would last, especially now that the fridges weren't working. In fact, when they got home, the first thing they would need to do was empty the meat from the freezer and begin bottling it in sealed jars.

In the past, John had always dreaded heading to places like Walmart on the weekends because of the hordes of annoying shoppers. Entering the Publix, he felt that same feeling as masses of shapes hurried about the dark store. There were only three carts left and John had to rush to grab one.

Moving from aisle to aisle was slow. It hadn't been more than a few hours since the electricity had stopped and already most of the shelves were picked clean. He knew why too. A regular power outage wasn't unheard of and rarely sent anyone rushing to clear out the store shelves, but when you added the stalled cars and lack of communication, the first signs of panic had already begun to settle in.

The lack of power was also slowing things down since it was hard to see more than a few feet in front of you, let alone what was on the shelves. Angry voices nearby filled the air as fights broke out over the few remaining items.

John headed straight for the drink aisle and scooped up as many two-gallon water jugs as he could find. The human body could go weeks with minimal food, but only days without water, which made that a priority. Once home, he would empty what was in the pipes to fill the bathtub and as many buckets as possible before the water pressure finally gave out. Afterward, he could always use a clean garden hose to drain the water heater in the basement if push came to shove.

Now that he had a good number of two-gallon jugs, John headed for the canned food section. Beans, pasta, corn, spam, vegetable soup. He needed to make sure his family got the widest array of vitamins and minerals. Many preppers concentrated on foods that were easy to store without thinking of a balanced diet. In the old days, sailors crossing the Atlantic had often succumbed to scurvy until they realized it was caused by a lack of vitamin C. It would only be a question of time before illnesses like scurvy that had been far behind them began to rear their ugly heads once again.

He then stocked up on salt, sugar and cooking oil. These were other common items often overlooked in emergencies.

It took an excruciating thirty minutes before John's cart was filled to capacity. Next he would have to wait in a twisting line for the cash. And cash was the right word, since credit and debit cards were completely useless. He was amazed at how many people were forced to leave empty-handed because credit was all they'd brought. The other thing that amazed him was how the tenuous threads of law and order still hung in the air. Those angered shoppers without cash left shooting off little more than their mouths. They threatened lawsuits and all manner of nonsense, but not one of them tried to steal the food. How long that veneer of civility would last, John could only guess. It would end when grumbling bellies began to take charge of people's behavior.

A woman in front of him with two small boys and a girl was visibly shaken. Either her husband was stranded at work or she was a single mom, trying to weather this crisis alone. John's heart went out to her. She turned to him and smiled weakly.

"Crazy, isn't it?"

He nodded. "Yeah, I hoped something like this would never happen."

"There are so many rumors flying around I just don't know what to believe."

He glanced in her cart and saw fruits, vegetables and three heads of lettuce. His heart sank even further. She'd fumbled an opportunity to stock up on some useful supplies by grabbing perishables. Course he couldn't blame her. Most people didn't have a clue what they needed in such situations.

"I hate to say it, but I think it's as bad as they're saying, maybe even worse."

Her face darkened with fear.

"I'm sorry," John said. "I know that isn't the kind of thing you wanted to hear, but it won't do you much good if I sugarcoat things."

"I just hope Craig's okay."

"Your husband?"

"Yeah, he's in Phoenix on business. The phones aren't working. I have no idea if he's lost power as well."

It was a good point. There was no telling how localized the problem was, but the further John had travelled—even just this morning—the more convinced he'd become that it was probably affecting the entire country.

"I'm sure he's fine," John offered, the words feeling hollow.

She smiled before advancing to the checkout girl.

His conversation with the woman had distracted him, but the closer John drew to the cash, the more outcries he became aware of. Even from people waving money around. And it didn't seem to be coming from frustrated customers trying to use credit cards. He wondered what was going on. After she was done, the woman with the perishables gave him one final look and all John could do was smile and mouth a silent prayer.

The checkout girl was sweeping each of John's items from right to left, rattling off prices as she went. Beside her, another girl recorded the numbers in a notepad. But something was odd about the numbers she was reading off. One can of corn, normally ninety-nine cents, was now five dollars. The water, once six dollars ninety-nine cents, was now fifteen dollars. Prices had doubled or in some cases quintupled. She hadn't even processed half of the items in John's cart before he was over the two-hundred-dollar mark.

"Wait a minute," he told the girl. "The price on two gallons of water is six ninety-nine, not fifteen dollars."

"I don't make the prices," she said matter-of-factly.

"Yes, but you're gouging people right when they need these things the most."

"I'm sorry you feel that way, sir, but this may be the last order we get this week. It's not me, it's my manager." She pointed to a mirror on the wall and the manager's office John knew was behind it.

What a weasel move. Hiking up prices during an emergency and making these young checkout girls take all the heat.

John had a difficult decision to make and he'd have to make it quickly. Given the state of things, there wasn't much chance of withdrawing any more money from the ATM. In fact, any money he had in the bank, as well as his 401k, had just gone up in smoke. He had ten thousand dollars' worth of gold pieces stashed at his house for just such a moment, except none of it would do him much good right now. It would still be a few days before people were ready to barter for goods and services. Cash and credit were so ingrained in the average mind that showing up with gold pieces would only add to the confusion. What would a teenage cashier know about the value of gold bullion?

A man behind John told him to hurry up.

"Sir?" the cashier asked. "Do you want the stuff or not? I've got other people in line."

He handed her his last two hundred dollars, gritting his teeth. Yes, he could take his chances at another grocery store or maybe even a mom-and-pop shop, but who was to say he'd have any more luck there?

Fuming, John left the store, pushing the cart filled mostly with the jugs of water and a few cans of food. He made it back to the Blazer to find Diane behind the wheel, looking nervous. Even though it was still early in the morning, the windows were opened a crack to let in some air.

John scanned the surrounding area to make sure it was safe to open the rear cargo hatch. Diane opened the window further and tossed him the keys. After loading everything onboard, John went to the driver's side and climbed in. Diane had already slid over to the passenger seat.

"The expression on your face tells me it wasn't pretty in there," she said. Emma and Gregory were asleep in the back seat.

"I didn't need this," he said, removing the S&W and handing it to her. "Things were about as orderly as one could expect under the circumstances." He then told her about his run-in with the cashier and the price gouging he'd experienced.

He started the engine and drove away.

"I can't say I'm all that surprised," she said.

John didn't agree. "A small convenience store I can understand, but a big chain?"

"When times are tough, people get greedy. In the end, no one was shooting the place up."

"Not yet," John said as he headed for home. "But it's only a question of time."

Chapter 9

Once home, John got out and manually opened the garage door while Diane drove Betsy in. The kids were awake by now, expressing how strange it felt to be missing class. Emma was staring off into the distance, likely also missing Brandon.

All of them helped bring the water and food inside. After that, John called a family meeting.

"Your mother and I need to make a decision," he told them.

The mood grew somber. He took the next several minutes to explain to all of them as best he could that the country and possibly a chunk of the planet had either been hit by a solar flare or an electromagnetic pulse. John had begun prepping three and a half years ago, so those terms were very familiar to each of them. John's preps had been geared toward a wide array of natural and man-made disasters, an EMP being only one of them. There were plenty of ways the country could implode, or explode, depending how one viewed it. A total collapse of the financial system, civil wars over gun control, meteor strikes, earthquakes, even alien invasion had been discussed. Either way, being ready for a complete breakdown of law and order had been his focus.

In some ways, the cause was merely academic. The EMP, however, had represented the worst of the worst since in one fell swoop the country would be sent back to the mid-1800s. Even the simple loss of electricity could be devastating, let alone the loss of ninety-nine point nine percent of all transportation and perhaps a hundred percent of communication. These were networks which bound modern society together, helped to preserve order. Now that they were gone, the thought of what might come next was frightening.

Every so often as he spoke, the kids checked their phones to see if somehow they would miraculously switch back on. It was a normal impulse and John knew how addicted to technology the younger generation was. For these reasons he didn't say anything. Sooner or later they'd figure out their precious gadgets weren't coming back.

After he explained what he thought was happening, Gregory raised his hand.

"Say what's on your mind, son."

"What does it matter if we were hit by an EMP or a solar flare? The result is the same."

"That's a good point, but there is an important difference. One is a random act of nature that occurs roughly once every five hundred years. The other involves the detonation of a nuclear weapon high in the atmosphere, say three to four hundred miles up. If that's the case, we're probably at war and it could mean that foreign troops are headed our way."

"Unless they're already here," Diane said, under her breath. She'd been sitting quietly until then, scratching the red polish off her nails.

"That is a distinct possibility."

Emma shifted in her seat. "Dad, you're starting to scare me."

"Good," John said. "'Cause these are things we need to be prepared to face."

His wife was trying hard to bite her lip.

"So we need to make a decision but I'm open to hearing input from each of you. We have the reinforced bunker downstairs that can keep us protected and fed for about a month. We also have the cabin about ten miles east of Oneida where we could survive for a year or longer. The bunker, however, was really designed for short-term emergencies. The problem we're facing is the longer we remain in Knoxville, the more dangerous the situation may become. Most of the government agencies that have wargamed a possible EMP attack suggest that within ninety-six hours the shock will begin wearing off as folks begin to get hungry. As we've talked about before, the average household only has enough provisions for a couple of days."

Emma shrugged. "I don't like the idea of abandoning all our things. What if they get things working again, but we're not here to protect the house? Someone could just come in and take all our stuff. Besides, what was the point of that submarine thingy you built in the basement if we're not going to use it?"

"She may have a point," Diane echoed.

The cabin wasn't nearly as comfortable as the house. John knew that as well as any of them, but he hoped it wasn't secretly factoring into their decision. He turned to Gregory who looked like he had something on his mind.

"What happens after those ninety-six hours you talked about?" Gregory asked. "Will it be too dangerous to leave?"

"It shouldn't be. We have Betsy."

"I'll go with whatever you say," his son said.

"Doesn't it make more sense to stay a few days," Diane said, "and keep an eye on the situation outside? Besides, maybe the community could use our help."

That did make sense. "Okay, for now we'll stay a day or two and see how things progress. I'll keep Betsy fueled up and ready for an immediate evac in case things get hairy. That means there's an incredible amount of work to do. Gregory, run upstairs and begin filling the bathtubs in the master bedroom and the one next to your bedroom with water. Make sure the tub itself is scrubbed before you do so." He turned to Emma. "I need you and your mom to bring the water and canned food I bought down to the pod and place it in the pantry."

"Shouldn't we board up all the windows?" Diane asked.

"Not all of them. That'll be a dead giveaway that we're in here and have stuff worth taking. For now we want to blend in and look like any other house on the block. We'll also need to create a stash with some food and weapons and bury it in the backyard in case we're overrun."

"Overrun?" Emma was giving him a strange look, like he was being too paranoid.

"You wanted to stay in Knoxville, well, this is the price. There's a chance roving bands might form to loot and plunder. We have to be ready in case that happens."

"Your father's right." Diane turned to Emma. "Let me get out of this skirt and throw some jeans on before we get started."

John headed into his basement office for the gun safe he kept in the corner. From there he took out one of his two Ruger SR22 pistols and a box of Winchester .22 bullets.

He was heading back upstairs when Diane intercepted him.

"I thought you were getting changed?"

"I will," she said. "But first I'd like to know where you're going with that gun."

"Next door to have a friendly conversation with Al."

Chapter 10

John went out the back sliding door and hopped the fence into Al's backyard. He didn't want anyone in the neighborhood seeing him going back and forth. He'd already been less than pleased at having to parade Betsy around the whole community.

John knocked on Al's back door and his elderly neighbor peered out at him from the blinds. A second later he opened up.

"You had me frightened to death, John," Al said, holding a baseball bat.

"Bad guys don't knock," John told him as he entered. "I wanted to check in quickly with you and Missy. See how you're holding up."

"'Bout as good as one could expect under the circumstances." Al closed the door. "Did you find Diane and the kids?"

"They're back at the house, getting things ready."

"I thought you were leaving?"

"We've decided to stay. At least for now."

Al smiled. "No bug-out?"

"That tends to be a knee jerk response for many who like to be prepared for the worst, but it isn't always the best idea."

"You still won't tell me where your secret hideout is, will you?"

"I could, but then I'd have to—"

"Kill me," Al finished, laughing. "Yeah, I know. I think Missy and I would be better off here anyway. Least till this mess is straightened out."

The two men went into the kitchen. "That's part of why I'm here, Al. There aren't enough supplies at our place to support two extra mouths, I hope you understand."

"Perfectly."

"Getting ready for the worst can be a full-time job, which makes it hard when you can't give it all the hours it deserves."

"No need to explain. Your only job is to keep your own family safe, I get that."

"But that doesn't mean I can't give you a few simple pointers which might help."

Al got a glass out of the cupboard and turned the tap on. Cold water was still flowing and he filled the glass and brought it to his lips.

"Did you fill buckets up like I suggested?"

"I did," Al replied. "Including the bathtub."

"Good. I've got Gregory doing the same thing at our place now. But you need to be prepared for when the water stops and it will."

"Really?"

"At the very least, your water may become discolored or unsafe to drink and I wanna show you how to clean it." In some ways, Al was like the father John had never known. Taking a few minutes to help him out wasn't a waste. Somehow he felt it was his duty.

"What would you suggest?"

"If the color changes or you need to filter water with debris, best thing is to use a coffee filter. If you run out a t-shirt will also work. Next you wanna take an eye dropper and add eight drops of bleach per gallon of

50

water. Shake it well. Then smell the water. If it doesn't smell faintly of bleach you wanna add a few more drops, but never more than sixteen."

John went over to the back door. Al's place didn't have a sliding glass one, which was good. "Wedge a chair underneath the handle and nail the feet into the floor. Do the same with the door to the garage but be sure to remove anything from there you think you'll need."

"I've got some plywood and two-by-fours out there as well," Al said. "Should I put those over the front windows?"

"Not necessarily."

"Coming from Mr. Paranoid, a statement like that really surprises me."

John couldn't help but chuckle. "I can see that. But here's my thinking, Al. The best defense you can have in a situation like this is to blend in. If your house looks like Fort Knox, the bad guys will wonder what valuables you're guarding in here."

"We don't have much to steal."

"Maybe more than you think. Remember, right now paper money is quickly becoming toilet paper. I was at the Publix earlier and the prices for standard items have skyrocketed. Most of the shelves were already empty."

There was suddenly a worried look on Al's face, like all of this was becoming real. "My retirement savings."

John put a hand on his shoulder. "I'm sorry to say that's probably all gone. These days most of our money's nothing more than ones and zeros floating around in some computer system."

"I don't believe it," Al said, wiping a bead of sweat from his brow.

"I can't blame you. My purpose in coming over here wasn't to unnerve you. Most everyone out there's running around thinking it's only a matter of time before things

51

return to normal. I don't think they will, not for a while, and many people won't live to see that day. In another few days the reality's going to settle in and when it does, the situation might get ugly. I want you to be ahead of the curve, Al. You've been a good neighbor over the years and I want you to at least be somewhat prepared."

Al nodded, vaguely.

"Good. Now, after you've secured those entryways, you need to think of a safe place in the house you and Missy can flee to in a worst-case scenario."

"We do have that guest bedroom in the basement."

"Perfect! You're going to turn that into your safe room. Use that wood you mentioned to reinforce the door and the frame. Then add a doorjamb that you can bolt to the floor. Bring down a cache of food and water so you can wait out any bad guys who show up." John produced the Ruger SR22 and the box of ammo. "This here is your last resort and it sure beats the hell out of that baseball bat you're using now."

"Oh, John, you know I don't like guns."

"Yeah, I know, but liking's got nothing to do with it. If someone breaks in here and means you or Missy any harm, you need to be ready. A .22 caliber bullet won't cut a man in two, but it'll be enough to wound and maybe even kill." John took a minute to show Al the basics of how to use it. Loading the magazine, flicking the safety on and off, pulling the slide and how to control his breath when squeezing the trigger. "Once you're done, that safe room will become your new bedroom. No more sleeping upstairs. It'll take you too long to get down there if someone comes in the middle of the night. You finish all that and then if you have time you can start booby-trapping windows and doorways. Nail boards at the foot of every window, upstairs and down, are a nice easy deterrent. Use your imagination."

52

Al was holding the gun as though it were a venomous snake.

"Handle her well and with the respect she deserves and she won't bite you, I promise."

"Sounds like something my wife would say."

The two men laughed and John could only pray that Al would implement what they'd talked about.

Chapter 11

John, Diane and the kids busied themselves over the next few hours fortifying the house. The strategy was similar to what John had recommended for Al. The truth of the matter was, if bad guys wanted to get into your house, nothing was going to stop them. You might reinforce your front door and add ballistic security glass, but what good would all that do when someone drove a truck in through your living-room wall?

John recalled seeing house-to-house searches conducted in Iraq. Many of the families there lived behind walls with strong gates and the Marines had simply knocked the gates down by smashing into them with their Humvees. If there was a will, there was a way. That was what made John's approach somewhat different from many of his colleagues in the prepping community. Funneling intruders into designated kill zones was part of his strategy. Forget trying to keep them out. Wound them getting in with razor wire around the inside edge of windows and sharpened nail boards designed to pierce all but the toughest boots. Then lead them down a hallway where the barrel of a shotgun awaited them.

Ironically, John's strategy meant slightly breaking his own rules. The sliding door and windows at the back of the house would all be boarded up on the inside and out. The front of the house—the side visible to the average passerby—would look normal. Criminals who snuck around back would become discouraged and opt for knocking down the front door or breaking a window. If the first few obstacles didn't deter them, then John's next trick would surely do the job. A single hallway led from the front of the house to the kitchen and the basement. It was a nice choke point where John had installed a five-by-five-foot AR500 ballistic steel plate with a gun port and a slit allowing him to see. The metal plate was speced to withstand most small arms.

If that didn't stop or dissuade the intruders, then they could flee to the basement and the pod. The pod hatch was set in the floor behind a false wall. Anyone who chopped through the basement door and came after them would find nothing but an empty room. Of course, these were scenarios John filed away under the absolute worst case. It was his neighbors he worried about the most.

A shed in his backyard held most of the wood and other building material left over from various construction jobs he'd been on. Mounting the plywood boards over the back windows and sliding door took the most time, especially since it was similarly reinforced on the interior as well. Gregory helped him, while Emma worked on the nail boards.

For her part, Diane emptied the freezer, salvaging what she could. Last year they'd purchased a Heartland Wood Cookstove, a beautiful work of art that harkened back to the pioneering days of the 1800s. This was where Diane would operate the pressure canner. The pod in the basement already had a pantry with canned meat, vegetables and fruits. But this would allow them to preserve most everything from their deep freezer that wasn't processed. The kids liked boxed pizzas and a few of them were left over from Diane's trip to the grocery store before the EMP hit. For efficiency, they'd decided to start with the food that would go bad first.

Bugging out, if it came to that, did raise another set of challenges. Sure, he, Diane and the kids all had their bug-out bags packed and ready to go, but what else would they be tempted to bring with them in the event they had to flee? Diesel for the truck was a must, along with as much food and water as they could carry. Then there were the medical supplies and a whole host of other considerations that were enough to make your head spin.

John kept water and some food in the truck already, along with the row of five-gallon jerrycans filled with diesel on the back. If they had to hurry, they could simply grab their bug-out bags and be gone within minutes.

With the rear windows and doors secure and the sharpened nail boards completed, John and the kids worked at attaching close to fifty feet of razor wire along the inside window frames. For that, each of them wore stainless-steel cut-resistant gloves and took their time to ensure no one got hurt. John's basic medical supplies consisted of sterile pads and gauze, cotton and medical tape, and compresses as well as hydrogen peroxide— enough to treat most any scrapes, cuts or wounds—but he had to keep in mind there wasn't any emergency room to go to anymore if things were more serious, so the best bet was to avoid getting hurt in the first place.

Just as he'd suggested to Al, John wanted his family to sleep in the pod. A hand-cranked air filtration system would help provide them with the oxygen they would need.

Beat after a physically and emotionally exhausting day, John was looking forward to grabbing some sleep. Diane and the kids were already in the pod unrolling their sleeping bags. Using a battery-powered Colman lantern,

John went to the gun safe he kept in his office and removed his Colt AR-15, along with his MCR1 Condor Tactical Vest that contained four thirty-round polymer magazines. Next he grabbed his PVS-14 nightvision monocle and walked through the house to ensure it was secure. Confident the house was properly locked down, John headed for the pod. Among the items he was carrying, the nightvision was one of the most important. If looters entered the house at night, he wanted to be able to see them before they saw him.

Chapter 12

By day two, for many the reality of the situation still hadn't sunk in. Standing on his front step, John saw a large group of his neighbors and their children having a cookout in the middle of the street. Some of them had rolled out three propane barbecues in a line and were making hot dogs and hamburgers. Next to it was a table with cases of soda. Bill Kelsaw, a neighbor from two houses down, waved John over. He was wearing a tall white chef's hat and flipping meat patties. Reluctantly John approached, not sure he wanted anything to do with what was going on.

"You want a burger?" Bill asked, smiling.

"What is all this?"

Bill looked at him as though he'd just landed from another planet. "John, it's the block party. Have you already forgotten?" Bill was having a great time. Behind him, kids were playing and shouting in the noonday sun. More neighbors had brought up folding chairs and begun chatting with one another. Then John spotted Al and Missy, mingling in the crowd.

Could he have already finished those preps on his own? John wondered.

"We're not gonna let some power outage ruin a yearly ritual," Bill was saying. "Hey, John, why don't you bring

Diane and the kids down? I'm sure they'd love to have a bite and enjoy themselves. John?"

"Huh, no, I don't think so."

Bill stopped flipping burgers long enough to put a hand on John's shoulder. "Let your hair down, man, and live a little."

Bill was seventy now, a child of the Sixties. As long there was a drink in his hand and he was having fun then nothing else seemed to matter. He hated anyone or anything that threatened to bring down his high.

"I feel like I'm dreaming," John said, looking around him.

"Hey, I've lived through all kinds of outages, my man. Ice storms, earthquakes. You name it, I've done it. You know the one thing I learned, John?"

"No, what's that, Bill?"

"You can't let Mother Nature control you." Smoke rose up from a row of burning patties. "Oh, damn," Bill said, flipping them again and realizing they'd become hockey pucks. Bill scooped them off the grill and tossed them into a trash bin beside him.

The sight of such waste, especially under the circumstances, was almost too much to bear. "In a week from now you'll be digging through the trash to eat those burgers."

Bill stopped, stunned. "Excuse me?"

"Are all of you living in some kind of fantasy land? Don't you see what's going on?"

The look on Bill's face was that of someone dealing with a madman.

"Now take it easy, John. Is this about the burgers I threw out? They were burnt, no one's gonna want them."

"Haven't you wondered, Bill, why none of the cars are running? Why the phones are all dead?"

59

"I have, John, and no one here knows what's happening because the TV's not working either. That tends to happen when the power goes out."

"I was near the interstate yesterday after it happened and you know what I saw?"

Bill shook his head, looking like he didn't want to have this conversation anymore.

"I saw thousands of stranded motorists abandoning cars that no longer worked and walking down what had become a parking lot."

Bill didn't say anything.

"Something terrible has happened, Bill, and to the degree that it's possible, I believe I'm prepared to handle what's coming. Are you?"

John walked away, but he didn't go home. He went over to Al, who was sitting in a folding chair next to his wife, drinking a beer.

A guilty look spread over Al's face, like a child who hadn't done his homework.

"Hey, Al. Hi, Missy."

"Hi, John," Al said, as Missy nodded hello. "Beautiful afternoon, isn't it?"

"It is. Did you manage to make any headway on what we spoke about yesterday?"

"I did," Al said. "Still plenty to do. Was going to do some more after the block party's done."

John smiled. "Okay, Al. Just let me know if you need a hand."

"Will do."

As he turned to leave, Missy said, "Why don't you send Emma and Gregory out for some hot dogs and drinks? I'm sure the other neighborhood kids would love to see them."

60

That was when John spotted Brandon, the young man he'd seen with Emma yesterday. He was sitting by Rose Myers' maple tree, looking sad and lonely.

When John got back to the house, an argument was in progress. Diane and Emma were shouting back and forth at one another. It was unusual to hear fighting in their household. He'd tried to teach the kids that being calm and collected was the best approach.

Diane was at the top of the stairs. "Will you talk to your daughter?"

"What's the problem?"

"She wants to go to the block party."

John shook his head. "I was just there. None of them have a clue how serious this is."

Emma poked her head out of her room. "I don't see why we're locked up in this house like prisoners. People are having fun outside and I'm stuck in Alcatraz."

"We're doing this for your own safety," John said. He turned to Diane. "The less in touch with reality those people outside are, the more it jeopardizes our own security."

"You don't think any of them would try and take what we have?" Diane asked, worried.

"Who can say for sure? Hunger can do crazy things to people. But more importantly, if the neighborhood isn't a united front, we'll be easy pickings for roving gangs looking to raid supplies."

From her room Emma said, "Look outside. They *are* a united front, Dad. We're the ones on the outside."

Diane bit her lip. "I hate to say it, but she might have a point. If we intend to stay, even for a little while, alienating ourselves from the neighbors might come back to haunt us."

61

John sighed. Under the circumstances, the willful neglect that was going on outside went against everything he held dear, but they did have a point. Adaptability and being able to swallow your pride for the greater good could spell the difference between life and death. History was littered with the bodies of men who'd stuck to their principles and died from inflexibility. He swallowed hard, knowing that putting on a smile while the world around him slowly boiled over would be difficult, but if the community was going to come together to make decisions in the future, he didn't want to be left on the sidelines.

Chapter 13

Outside, not long after, Al tapped John on the shoulder and offered him a Budweiser.

John took it and twisted off the cap. "I think we should begin setting up some sort of committee."

"What for?"

"Might not be long before we need to start making decisions collectively. It's always best not to wait for a crisis to know who's in charge."

Al nodded. "I suppose it can't hurt to start spreading the word. I think Dan Foster used to work in the mayor's office before he started his own law practice. I could have a chat with him."

John took a bite of a hot dog and set it down on a paper plate. "Hmm, hold off on talking to Dan just yet."

"Oh, did you hear what happened on Silversted?" Al asked.

"No, I didn't."

Al ran a wrinkled hand through what was left of his graying hair. "The street runs parallel to the interstate and apparently yesterday a few dozen folks came knocking on doors, asking for a place to stay for the night."

"You mean the ones who were stranded on the highway?"

"Looks that way. I believe they were all taken in, fed and given a place to sleep."

John took another swig of his beer, touched although worried at the same time.

"After the power went out, a bunch of them continued on to work while the rest turned around and headed home. It was the ones who got all the way into town and found their offices closed who got stuck when darkness fell. In a situation like this, that's all most folks want anyway, right? To find a way home."

"What about the police?" John asked. "Any word on whether they've been out at all?"

"Sally Wright from Maple Lane was saying she saw a number of them in groups of five or six. On some sort of patrol. Says she asked, but they didn't know what had happened to cause this."

"Didn't know or wouldn't say?"

"Hmm, not sure."

"How were the cops getting around?" John asked.

"Bikes."

"That makes sense. I wonder how they get anyone to the station though."

Al laughed. "I wondered that myself. I guess the bad guys ride on the handlebars or something. But Sally also said she went to over to the Publix this morning to get a few things and found the shelves had been stripped bare."

"That so?" John said, not the least bit surprised. Maybe now the seriousness of the situation would begin to sink in.

Over by a group of kids playing horseshoes on a neighbor's lawn, John spotted Emma. She was with Brandon and the two of them were sitting on folding chairs, giggling.

Al followed John's glance. "It's a fact of life, you know."

"What's that?"

"Falling in love. Happens to us all. The lucky ones at least."

"I know, Al. Emma's a good kid. I trust her implicitly. It's this boy I'm not sure about."

"Well, they're out in the open when they could be hiding out of sight. That oughta count for something." Al looked down at the empty beer in his hand. "Want another one?"

John shook his head and Al sauntered off to the cooler.

He wasn't alone for more than a few seconds before he heard a voice behind him.

"They're quite fond of each other, aren't they?"

He turned and found Tim Appleby, Brandon's father.

John nodded. "They seem to be. Although it can't hurt to keep an eye on them. Kids do have a habit of doing silly things."

"Couldn't agree more," Tim said, smiling. "We were young too once."

John didn't know much about Tim, other than that he worked as a musician, playing piano in hotel bars downtown.

Tim rubbed his hands together, twiddling his fingers as though he was prepping for a recital. "I've been hearing from some of the neighbors that you think this is gonna last more than a few days."

"I know it will, Tim, but no one is really willing to accept that yet."

"Can you blame them? I spent a stint living up in Montreal back in the late Nineties. In '98 we were hit with one of the worst ice storms in history. Two million people without power for a full week. And let me tell you something. I never had so much fun in my life."

John shook his head. "Yeah, I heard about that. Were there cops on the streets?"

"All over," Tim said. "I've never seen so many cop cars. A few incidents of firewood and generator thefts, but overall people muscled through it. If they can last a week, then so can we."

"Maybe, Tim, but this isn't going to last a week. Won't even last a month. I know it's hard to believe, but there's a very good chance it could be months, maybe even a year before things start returning to normal. Until then we're getting a crash course in what it was like to live in the 1800s."

The color faded from Tim's face.

"I know the party mode is still in full swing," John went on. "And hey, everyone handles things in their own way, but sometime in the next twenty-four to forty-eight hours, we're gonna need to have a meeting for the residents of Sequoyah Hills to sort out issues of food and security. Tactically speaking, we've got the river at our backs. It wouldn't be terribly difficult to create a series of checkpoints so we can be sure who's coming into our neighborhood." John suddenly remembered something. "You own an old Mustang, don't you?"

"Yeah, a 1973. Just finished detailing her."

"Have you tried running her since yesterday?"

"No, I just assumed she wouldn't work."

"I suspect she'll run just fine. In fact, if push comes to shove she may come in handy. I've got a '78 Blazer myself which still runs just fine. At the meeting, we'll need to see who else has an older car that we could use."

"That makes sense. Let me talk to some people and see what I can get going."

"All right. Thanks, Tim."

"Don't mention it." Tim paused. "There was another reason I came to speak with you."

"I'm all ears."

66

"I just wanted to let you know that Brandon is a good kid."

"I'm sure he is."

Tim smiled and walked away. Diane came up to John a few minutes later and wrapped her arms around him.

"You finding the same thing I am?" she asked.

"Denial, you mean?"

She let out a worried laugh.

"Yeah," he said. "But it's not all bad. I've been spreading the word that we need to have a meeting for all residents of Sequoyah Hills."

"And people seem receptive?"

"So far. Al was telling me the Publix was completely cleaned out. It's only a question of time before the hunger sets in."

He saw the concern growing on her face.

"We're still in a good spot, honey," he told her. "No need to worry. We've got plenty of food, a safe place to sleep and a house that's nicely fortified. Compared to the rest of these free-spirited partygoers, we're well ahead of the curve. Besides, if the crap really does hit the fan, we've always got plan B."

Diane hugged John tighter.

"I spoke with Brandon's father just now," he said.

She looked up at him. "And?"

"Seemed nice enough. Told me about a disaster he lived through up in Montreal years ago and what a great time he had."

She laughed. "Oh, boy."

"He has a '73 Mustang that might still work."

Her eyes narrowed. "I sense a but in there somewhere."

John's wife knew him too well. "Tim's a musician."

"So?"

"Before yesterday it wouldn't have mattered. But as things progress, anyone without a useful skillset will be in real danger."

Chapter 14

The next morning, John unsealed the hatch and emerged from the pod to a loud booming noise. It sounded like it was coming from upstairs. He climbed back down the ladder into the pod and got his S&W, checking to make sure the magazine was full.

"What is it, John?" Diane sounded concerned.

"Not sure," he told her. The kids were awake too now. "Wait down here till I give the okay. Seal the hatch behind me after I leave."

"Need some backup?" Gregory asked.

"Thanks, bud, but not this time."

"Be careful," Diane said as he climbed out again.

No sooner was he topside than he heard the pounding again. John slid back the false wall and headed upstairs. Early-morning light trickled in from outside. Whoever was making that racket was sure persistent. Once upstairs, he saw that it was coming from the front door. He slipped into the living room and peeked out through the window. Al was there, hammering his fist a final time before walking away. John hurried and pulled open the front door.

"Al," he said, sliding the S&W into his drop-leg holster. "If I didn't know any better I might have shot you."

His neighbor looked out of breath and John knew right away it was serious. "Come quick."

They ran down to the end of the street. A crowd had gathered, many of them in their pajamas. Some of the older women were wearing robes pulled tightly around them.

"What's going on?" John asked, breathing deeply.

One of his neighbors named Peter Warden, a gym teacher over at the junior high, was coming toward them with an armful of blankets. "We heard shots this morning and saw figures with guns running through the neighborhood."

Some of the neighbors milling around were armed with deer rifles and pistols.

"They hit two houses at the end of the street," Al said.

"Who's they?" John asked, confused.

Peter shrugged. "No one knows. Men with guns. And they ransacked Paul Hector's place."

"Who else?" John asked.

"Tim Appleby."

John's heart dropped. Emma would be a wreck once she found out. "Is everyone okay?" He was following Peter now as he approached the Hector family home. All five family members were sitting on the front stoop. Peter handed them each a blanket and then turned back to John. "Everyone here is accounted for, but there's still no word from Tim or his family."

"How many of them are there?"

"Four," Peter answered. "Tim, his wife Kay, son Brandon and daughter Natalie."

John motioned for Al to follow him and the two hurried down to the corner of Willow Creek and Pine Grove where the Appleby home was located. A handful of neighbors were coming in and out of the house. The

70

garage door was open. John entered from there and noticed at once Tim's car was gone.

"That's what I was afraid of," John said.

Al stopped to catch his breath. "But how could anyone steal a car that didn't work?"

"He had a '73 Mustang. When the EMP hit, it knocked out anything with a microchip. Older cars, like his and Betsy, were largely immune."

They entered the house. John figured whoever had done this was long gone, but drew his pistol anyway. You never knew if a bad guy had been wounded during the assault and was waiting in a closet somewhere. He checked behind him and saw Al with the Ruger SR22. "Keep your finger off that trigger until it's time to shoot," he told his neighbor. He stopped before a handful of others assembled in the house. "Has anyone conducted a thorough search of the house yet?" he asked.

A teenaged boy raised his hand. "I looked upstairs and didn't see anyone."

"Okay, each of you, go in the kitchen and grab a weapon of some kind. Go in groups of two and start a fresh search from the basement up. Keep an eye out for places in closets and behind doors where someone could be hiding. Al and I will start upstairs and meet you back here on the main floor."

They spent the next ten minutes tearing the house apart without finding a soul. The place looked like it'd been ransacked. A jewelry box lay on the floor, its contents spilled out like the guts of a slaughtered calf. A sinking feeling was building in John's gut. Whoever had done this might have taken Tim and his family hostage.

They reached the main floor and continued searching, but it was already clear they weren't going to find anyone. The other group emerged from the basement. "Anything?" John asked.

They shook their heads.

"Maybe they managed to escape on their own," Al suggested. "Got in the car and drove as far away as they could."

John nodded. "I hope you're right."

Chapter 15

John sent a group to check the remaining houses on Willow Creek and call whoever was still inside. It was nearly ten o'clock by the time all the families had assembled. There were thirty-two houses on their street and at least two to four people from each house. Only one of them stood empty. The Wilsons had moved out in the early spring before selling—Andrew Wilson was a doctor and could afford to keep the second home. Right now Andrew's medical knowledge would have been handy to their little group.

A ladder from Paul Hector's garage would be John's podium. It was important that everyone could see him clearly, even though the thought of taking charge of these people still didn't sit well with him. John was a man who normally kept to himself, minding his own business. Al was one of the few neighbors he spoke to and even Al knew very little about John's prepping lifestyle. Without being too cloak-and-dagger about it, secrecy was an important part of successful preps that many overlooked or flat-out ignored. And John understood why. You spent loads of time and money to weather a SHTF event and couldn't let anyone but your family know any of the details.

Al cleared his throat.

Dozens of eyes looked back at John. He swallowed. "As many of you already know," he began, "two houses in our neighborhood were attacked last night. The Hectors aren't real hurt, but we're still not sure what happened to the Applebys."

Emma cried out and covered her face with her hands. Diane pulled her close. He wished he'd had more time to tell her beforehand, but things were moving fast now and time was of the essence.

"We've searched the house and there are no signs of the family or the ones who did this. We know they were armed and were looking for food and other valuables. Our hearts and prayers go out to Tim and his family. Let's hope they're safe and sound."

Some members of the crowd bowed their heads and whispered silent prayers. Others stood stunned as though this were all some movie they were watching on TV.

"I'd just spoken to Tim yesterday about organizing such a meeting, but hoped it wouldn't have been under these circumstances." John sighed, hating this next part. "I know wild rumors have been floating around since the power went out about what's causing all this. I also know many of you are keenly aware this isn't your ordinary grid-down scenario. I spent close to ten years in the military, experiencing things I don't care to mention so none of you would ever have to. Seems all that was for naught. I believe that two days ago our country was hit with something called an EMP."

The crowd began to murmur.

"In short, gamma rays from the detonation of a high-altitude nuclear missile caused an oscillating electric current and in turn an electromagnetic pulse which wiped out all electronic devices within a huge blast radius. A single missile exploding four hundred miles over Kansas would be enough to knock out every electrical device over the continental United States. Apart from a solar flare, I can't think of anything else that would stop cars and fry cells phones and computers all at once."

"We've been nuked?" Peter said incredulously. He'd been the one to bring blankets to the Hectors this morning.

"If I'm right, then it looks that way," John told him. "But I wanna caution all of you that without some sort of confirmation from the military, we shouldn't assume we're at war. I tried telling you folks earlier, but my words fell on deaf ears."

"It's so hard to believe," a neighbor named Rose Myers exclaimed.

"But we haven't seen the worst of it yet," John went on. "Most homes in major cities have a few days' worth of food and water. Once that's done, it's only a question of time before the rule of law completely breaks down."

"The water's already stopped," Al said. "Tried my tap this morning and only a few drops came out."

"There's still water in your pipes and in your water heaters," John said. "It's important when we're done here that at least one member of your household be in charge of collecting what's there. It's also important moving forward that any water consumed be boiled first, since the treatment facility likely stopped working before the water was cut off. Now we can't save all of Sequoyah Hills, but we can at least help protect those of us on Willow Creek Drive. I propose we immediately move to elect a committee of six men and women to make decisions on securing our street."

"Why don't we just vote on everything?" Peter asked.

John shook his head. "Having to assemble everyone on the street to make decisions will cripple us. It's best to have a small governing body who can then disseminate the decisions.

"Each member of the committee will be responsible for a different area. Food-gathering, water filtration, security. That sort of stuff. The remaining residents will be divided under committee leaders and tasked with carrying out specific jobs."

"Sounds to me from the way you're talking like you won't be in the committee?" Al asked John.

"I'd prefer not to," he told them. "But I'm happy to help in any other way I can."

Paul Hector came forward. "My family was almost murdered last night. I had to hand over all the food we had to criminals. What'll happen when they return and I have nothing left to give them? We need someone with military experience on the committee."

Everyone present agreed. John shrugged. He could see Diane in the crowd and she didn't seem thrilled by the idea, but there was little else they could do. Things were getting worse, no doubt, but the situation wasn't bad enough to bug out and leave all these people to fend for themselves. Not yet at least. John swallowed hard. "For now, I'm happy to act as an advisor to the committee until we secure the area."

That seemed to satisfy people.

"Willow Creek is a cul-de-sac," John went on. "There's one way in by car and one way in by foot from the park at the other end of the street. I suggest while we're assembling the committee and having our first meeting, the rest of you push stalled cars and trucks in the way to create a roadblock where Willow Creek meets Pine Grove and a barricade and checkpoint at the cul-de-sac by the park." He looked to Peter. "Would you mind overseeing that?"

Peter nodded. "I'm on it."

John turned to Al. "Now we gotta figure out who's on this committee."

Chapter 16

There had been talk of voting people onto what was quickly becoming known as the Willow Creek committee, but with everyone scrambling to create the barricades and gather what water they could, it was left to John to decide.

Gregory had joined the group at the corner of Willow Creek and Pine Grove while Emma had disappeared into the house. News of the attack on Brandon and his family had been hard on her.

"I don't like having this much power," John told Al and Diane, who had followed him back to the house.

"I know, honey, but it won't be for long."

John wasn't convinced of that.

"You tried to back out and they wouldn't let you," Al told him. "It's not like you were vying for it."

"That's the problem. When people are frightened, they have a tendency to hand over all their power to the first person who stands up."

Al put his hands on his hips. "Well, we better get to work figuring out who's on this committee before they elect you king."

All three of them laughed uneasily.

"I don't want anyone with a political background," John said.

"Is that why you didn't want me talking to Dan Foster when I mentioned him during the block party?"

"That was one reason. I know he worked in the mayor's office once, but the last thing we need is anyone who'll be inclined to game the system for their own advantage."

"Well, that's rather cynical," Diane said.

"I'm not saying Dan's corrupt," John clarified. "Let's face it, whether we like it or not, politics nowadays has become a game. Doesn't really matter if you're working for the local mayor or the president. I simply want to avoid anyone who'll be inclined to play politics when what we really need in the next few days is solid action."

"I see your point," Al said and Diane nodded too. "We also don't want people who've never had to make a hard decision in their entire lives."

"Good point," John said. "Opinionated is all right too, so long as they can provide a solution to the problem they bring up. I don't want a dysfunctional group of people complaining to one another. I think we need to break this down into sectors and recommend someone who has experience in that given area."

Diane seemed to think that was a great idea. "Food management, clean water."

"Those are two big ones," John said. "We also need security, health."

"What about someone to liaise with other communities and local authorities?" Al added.

"And information," Diane said. "People want to know what's going on in other parts of the city, maybe even the country. We should have a group dedicated to gathering info and keeping the rest of us updated."

John nodded. "Yeah, and I hate to say it, but that information they collect will need to be vetted first."

"Really, John?" Al said, recoiling. "That sounds an awful lot like censorship to me."

"I think the First Amendment's important, believe me, but with so many rumors flying about, it doesn't do us any good to spread anything that we can't substantiate. I don't want these people believing the National Guard's about to swoop in and save us if most of the troops have gone home to protect their own families."

"We'll be heading down a slippery slope," Al said, looking at both of them.

Al was right and John knew it. "I'm afraid we're a lot further down than we're willing to concede just yet, Al. The attack last night was likely little more than a probe. Whoever was behind it believes they've found a nice soft target and we need to make sure they're thoroughly disappointed when they return."

"So who do you think should fill each of those positions?" Al asked.

John looked down at the folded envelope he was using to take notes. "Let's start with health since we likely already have issues to deal with there. Do we know of anyone who's a doctor?"

"Dr. Wilson, but he's gone," Al said.

John nodded.

"Edward Long's wife Patty is a nurse," Diane said, waving a finger. "She taught me how to tie a tourniquet last year."

"Okay," John said, marking her down. "That could work. Her first responsibilities would be to chart and document the list of residents with special medical needs. She can also start training a handful of people under her to help the sick and wounded and bring medicine to the elderly and infirm."

Diane looked suddenly grim. "You know the sick and the elderly will probably be the first to go, given the state of things."

Stark as it was, Diane did have a point. "It'll be unavoidable unless we can get the medicine we need."

"You heard Sally Wright, the grocery store shelves were already picked clean," Al said in despair. "I can only imagine what the pharmacies must look like."

"That's where security and liaison come in," John told them with a sly grin.

Diane threw him a quizzical look.

"One security detachment will be responsible for going out to pharmacies to procure what we need."

"And what if they're empty?" Al asked.

But John had an answer for that. "Then the liaison office will use their connections within the surrounding communities to identify who has the meds we need and set up a way to barter for it."

Diane laughed. "Willow Creek is quickly becoming its own little country."

"For now," John said. "I'll take over security and handpick a half-dozen men and teenage boys that I can deputize. As for the liaison officer, you're one of the most likeable guys on the block, Al. Maybe that's a role you could fill."

Al blushed and clapped John on the back. "With all the time I spent watering my garden, I was sure you woulda made me the groundskeeper." His belly shook as he rattled off a phlegmy laugh. "I sold fertilizer for forty years, so slinging crap won't be anything new for me."

"So that leaves food, water and information," John said, glancing at his notes.

Diane shook her head. "Here's the thing. Some of us will have more food than others do. John, I hope you're not suggesting we put all our food together and have it doled out by the committee."

"There's another slippery slope," Al said, "that'll lead straight to Communist Russia. People will wonder why they should push themselves when the state provides everything they need."

The comparison frustrated John. "That's not what I'm suggesting at all. Food management will keep track of what families have less than a week's worth of food left. We can then have that family provide items we can use to barter with another community or see if anyone on the street is willing to help them out."

"What about water?" Diane asked.

"That group will need to set up collection and filtration stations, possibly connected to eavestroughs to gather overflow. Worst-case scenario they'll need to sort out heading down to the Tennessee River and getting it that way."

"Any candidates come to mind?" Al said.

"Sure, one comes right to mind for food management. Arnold Payne imported and exported dried fruits and nuts, so he should know something about keeping inventory lists and keeping track of what's coming and going. As for water, doesn't Susan Wheeler work for Knoxville sanitation?"

"I believe she did," Al said. "Guess all that leaves is information."

"That's a tricky one. Just like Dan Foster and the mayor's office, I don't want anyone who's ever worked for a newspaper."

"Really?" Diane said. "Someone like that would be perfect. In fact, Patty Long's daughter is studying journalism."

"Which makes her a double whammy," John shot back. "First off, I don't want two members of the same

81

family on the committee. Second, someone who's studying journalism will feel bound by the journalistic principle to inform the people, no matter how damaging that information might be. I know censorship is a touchy subject, but we're already facing an uphill battle. It won't help anyone's morale to hear that the government's been dissolved or that half the population is dead."

"Curtis Watkins worked for the Census Bureau," Al said.

John snapped his fingers and jotted Curtis' name down. "He'll be perfect. We want someone who'll gather and record the information they find without zealously trying to spread the word."

"At least not until the committee's voted on it," Diane said.

Both men nodded and John glanced down at his list again, not sure yet whether this experiment in self-governance would work or end in complete disaster.

Chapter 17

Most of the neighborhood was still moving stalled cars into position at both ends of the street and reinforcing the barricade with whatever they could find. John now had a committee list he would present, but before he did he wanted to make sure Emma was all right.

He found her in her bedroom, little more than a mound underneath her blankets. John settled at the end of her bed and nudged her.

Emma's head came out. Her eyes were ringed with red puffy circles. She sniffled and brought a tissue to her nose.

"Your mother said you wouldn't talk to anyone."

"What is there to say?"

"I know it doesn't look good for Brandon and his family, but I wouldn't expect the worst just yet."

Emma sat up and scrunched her hands together. "I can't help it, Dad, I'm just so worried. His house was ransacked. Mr. Hector and his family were nearly murdered."

"I know. I spent most of the morning going through both scenes. We searched Brandon's house top to bottom, honey, and didn't find a soul. But that isn't a bad thing. It means we also didn't find any signs that something bad happened to them."

"What if they were kidnapped?"

That was a distinct possibility and one that had occurred to John. It was a tactic Somali pirates in the Gulf of Aden often used. Except here, instead of demanding ransom from a shipping company, these pirates would demand it from the residents of Willow Creek in food and resources.

"I doubt that very much," he lied. "I'm sure they fled to a safe zone somewhere. Brandon's father did have one of the few cars on the street that still worked."

"Can we use Betsy to search for them?"

John frowned. "Honey, I know he's important to you, but what would that accomplish besides opening us to unnecessary harm? I'd be willing to bet they're heading for some sort of government rendezvous point. Maybe they caught wind of a special FEMA camp. You know, like the Superdome in New Orleans after Katrina?"

She didn't seem convinced and he couldn't blame her. With so much of the country's infrastructure knocked out, it was hard to be optimistic about any sort of rescue. "Right now there's nothing we can do about Brandon or his family. I can't promise you he's okay, but I can promise that if we don't all pitch in here and now, then we'll all be at risk. Those bad men who came by last night will probably come again."

Emma was scraping the polish off her nails, just like her mother did when she got nervous. "You're starting to scare me," she said.

"Your brother's out there now, helping to build barricades."

The front door opened and closed, then footsteps ran up toward them. It was Peter Warden. "Sorry to barge in, John. We've moved some vehicles into blocking positions by Pine Grove and near the park."

"Okay, good," John said. "Anything else?"

"Everyone's assembled outside, ready to go over your suggestions for the committee." Peter seemed to sense the unease within John. "None of us on Willow Creek have any military experience. That's why they look up to you. It's not a bad thing."

"I know. I just don't want to get used to it, that's all."

•••

The people assembled outside John's house represented all the residents of Willow Creek. They ranged in age from Claire and Tom Hodges' six-month-old daughter to Dorothy Klein, who had recently celebrated her eighty-second birthday. In all, he guessed there was close to a hundred of his neighbors gathered before him.

The ladder he'd used earlier outside Paul Hector's place had already been set up. He climbed up the first few rungs until he could see everyone and reached into his back pocket for the envelope where he'd written the names.

"The Willow Creek committee will consist of six members. I've made recommendations for each position based on skillsets and experience in each given area. If any of you would prefer not to have a role on the committee let me know and I'll scratch you off." John peered down at the jumble of pen marks and scratched-off names and began to read. "For food management I recommend Arnold Payne." John stopped and searched the crowd to find Arnold, who raised his hand and nodded. "You up for the challenge?" John asked.

"Anything I can do to help," he replied.

"Good to hear. For water management I recommend Susan Wheeler. I'll temporarily take charge of security until we can find someone else. Patty Long will be responsible for health. Al Thomson will be our liaison officer and Curtis Watkins will be in charge of gathering and disseminating information to the residents of Willow Creek."

John searched the crowd, eyeing each person he named. "If any of you don't feel up to performing your duties let me know as soon as possible so we can find a replacement."

Bill Kelsaw raised his hand.

"Yeah, Bill, what is it?"

"Al's our new liaison guy, but I'll be damned if I know what that means."

Others were nodding as well.

"Think of the liaison officer as a kind of diplomat. He'll be in charge of talking to any other local groups that have begun to organize like us. He can help negotiate mutual security, medical or food items to be bartered. He can also arrange borrowing certain skilled laborers we don't have. Welders, carpenters. That sort of thing."

John then quickly went through and explained the other roles and what their responsibilities would be.

When he was done, Arnold spoke up. "So what do we do now?"

"Now," John said, "we have our first meeting and figure out how to keep everyone on Willow Creek safe."

•••

The first meeting was held in Patty Long's house. All six members of the new committee sat around her antique dining-room table. The chairs weren't terribly comfortable, but that might encourage them to keep the socializing to a minimum.

All eyes turned to John and once again that wave of discomfort washed over him. He should have known the minute he'd first climbed that ladder in front of Paul Hector's place this morning that he was setting a dangerous precedent.

"We have a lot to do in a very narrow window of time," John told them. "So I suggest we get started. Generally speaking, all of you know your roles, but there are some specifics we need to cover. First things first, we'll need to create lists of the resources at our disposal. I suggest each of you get a good old-fashioned notepad and pen before we begin. Computers and tablets are gone now, so we might as well start getting used to it."

Nervous laughter sputtered from Susan and Curtis.

"Arnold, since you're in charge of food, you'll need to find out what families on the block are getting low on groceries. As I've mentioned before, the average household will be running out of food soon." John turned to Susan. "Water's even more crucial. I know you worked for the sanitation department, so none of this should be news to you. You'll need to get a team of five young people to help you collect and purify water. Set up a central reservoir somewhere so anyone on the street can get what they need." He then looked at Susan. "For you, a list of the street's most at-risk residents is a must. The elderly, diabetics, anyone taking medication. Those are the ones likely to go first if we can't get them the help they need. Once we know, we can start looking at ways to find pharmacies that haven't been looted already."

"Good luck," Curtis said. "I walked to the convenience store over on Harvard and it was boarded up. Peeked through to see if anyone was inside and all the shelves were empty."

"We'll think of something," John told them. "Al, you and I spoke earlier about your role as liaison. Once I've selected my security team, I'll assign one member to stay with you on your rounds of the local neighborhoods.

87

Start by looking for any sign of organization and if you find one, make sure to speak with the person in charge."

Al flashed his impossibly white teeth. "Will do."

"Am I forgetting anyone?"

"Uh, me," Curtis said, smiling. "Who am I gonna be, Robin Williams from *Good Morning, Vietnam*?"

They all burst out laughing, including John. "That would be nice, if we all had radios that worked. No, I think for now you should head out with Al and ask around to see what you can find out. Afterward, come to us with whatever you've discovered and we can all vote on which bits of information to pass along."

Curtis, Patty and Arnold were visibly uncomfortable with this.

"I think it's better to put it all out there," Patty said, "and let people decide for themselves what's important."

"I'd have to agree," Arnold added. "We don't want to start treating people like children, do we?"

"And what about unsubstantiated rumors?" John asked. He'd already started sketching out the neighborhood's defenses. "Surely those might lower morale."

"Or increase it," Curtis said. "I think we should take a vote on that right now."

The others seemed to be in agreement, except for Al.

"By show of hands it's four to two," Curtis said. "Besides, rumors are swirling around anyway, a few more can't hurt."

John knew otherwise, but kept his mouth shut. Much as he hated to admit it, there was often a valid reason why certain bits of information were withheld from the general public. The problem was everyone wanted to be in the know, so finding a place to draw that line was difficult. He hoped for the sake of Willow Creek and its inhabitants that Curtis and the others were right.

•••

After the meeting broke up and each member went to attend to the items they'd discussed, Al stopped John on his way out. "I'd say overall that went pretty well."

"Better than I expected," John replied. "I can't say I was all that surprised with their reaction toward the end."

"I had a similar one," Al said frankly. "Even though it might be the right thing to do, decisions like that take time."

"They take mistakes."

"How so?"

John frowned. "Protocol in the military wasn't built upon successes so much as they were built on mistakes. Usually those mistakes meant lives were lost."

"You think it could be that serious."

"I can't say just yet, Al. Depends what kind of information is floating around out there. What if word spreads that there's a relief camp with plenty of food and water set up a day's walk from here? How many might leave and never come back? Now suppose that camp doesn't exist, it's only a rumor put out there by someone with their head in the clouds and nothing better to do than fabricate stories out of thin air. Then we've lost valuable people over nothing."

"Why didn't you say that during the meeting?" Al asked.

"There wasn't any point. If I start looking like the heavy, coming down on the personal liberties everyone is still used to, then we might not get anything done. I don't have to be here, Al. I've got another place that's far away and safe and could likely see me through this mess. I'm here 'cause I couldn't stand the thought of leaving behind so many people in need."

89

"We appreciate that, John, we really do. But it's like you said. No one's really sure what's going on and none of them, including myself, are prepared just yet to give up the old ways of doing things."

"Trust me," John told him. "I get it. I'd been sending out feelers from the start about getting everyone on the street together for a meeting and none of them would have anything to do with it. They were more interested in eating hot dogs and drinking beer. It was only after we were attacked that they finally listened. That's human nature, I understand that. And it's precisely why I kept my mouth shut. You ever have kids, Al?"

There was suddenly a look of sadness in Al's eyes. "No, only a younger brother. Eight or nine years between us. But we don't talk anymore."

John laid a hand on his friend's shoulder. "I'm sorry to hear that. I'm sure you remember talking to him as a teenager, warning him to be careful, not drive too fast. How did that go?"

"They don't listen," Al admitted. "They don't ever think anything bad's going to happen, not to them at least."

"There you go. The sad truth is most of us don't really change. 'It'll never happen to me' soon becomes shock and horror when the men with guns show up. Which is precisely why I need to find the men and women who are going to man the barricades and keep us from being slaughtered like sheep."

"There's a visual," Al said, half smiling. "I'll go find Curtis and see where he wants to start reaching out to the other neighborhoods."

Chapter 18

Ten minutes later, John found the man he was looking for.

"I want you to be my head of security," he told him.

Peter Warden's eyebrows went up. "I'd be honored," he said, smiling.

The choice wasn't a difficult one for two reasons in particular. The first was that Peter was a gym teacher at the local junior high, which meant he was fit and had experience telling others what to do. The second and perhaps most important was something John had seen earlier when they had discovered the Applebys and Hectors had been attacked. John had told Peter to roll those stalled cars into position to create a barricade and Peter had done it enthusiastically and without questions. Those were the qualities John was looking for and he was thrilled when Peter accepted his offer.

"Have you ever served in the military or fired a weapon?" John asked.

"I shot at squirrels with a .22 on my grandfather's farm years back. Does that disqualify me?"

John grinned. "Not at all. I'm sure you have more experience with firearms than most of the kids we're going to recruit."

"Kids?" Peter stammered.

John nodded. "They pick up quick and tend to take directions from authority figures. You know what they say about teaching old dogs new tricks?"

Peter laughed. He was stout with a thick neck and strong limbs. The longer they chatted, the more comfortable John was becoming with his choice.

"The other committee members are going to be looking to fill out their teams as well, so we'll need to move fast. Including the two of us, I figure we'll need another twelve deputies. Two for each barricade, two for patrols, one in the crow's nest and their shift replacements."

"Crow's nest?"

John smiled. "You'll see. About weapons, we're gonna need to get half of the new recruits assigned straight away to scrounging up as many firearms as people can spare. I've got a couple Ruger SR22s, two Mini-14s and a Bushmaster AR-15 that I can donate. If we need to go on a run to Gold N Guns then so be it. I just hope there's still something left." John was quiet for a moment.

"What is it?" Peter asked.

"Oh, it's just that I've spent a few years preparing for an event like this, but only for my family. I assumed I'd bug out at the first sign of trouble. The scale is so much larger when you include dozens more people. I feel like it'll take years to get to a good place where we're feeling secure."

"After the attack this morning," Peter said, "I have a sneaking suspicion we don't have years, or even weeks."

"It could be hours. Which is why we need to move it. Go find seven fit men and women between, say, seventeen and twenty-five, preferably unmarried, and I'll do the same. If we get stuck we can always take a handful of older folks."

Peter tapped John on the chest. "Older folks. That would be us, partner."

•••

An hour later they met back in front of John's house. In the summer heat and scorching sun, his lawn was starting to show dry patches. So were some of the others on the block. But gone was a time when water would be wasted on such things.

Peter had done as John had asked and brought five young men and two women. For his part, John hadn't been as lucky. He'd only managed to find three teenaged boys, one young woman and three men in their late fifties. Seemed like the rest were on water or food duty. They would have to do for now. If a crack shot with a rifle turned up later in Patty's nursing candidates or in Al's liaison team, then John would recommend they make a swap. There was something incredibly informal and rushed about the whole thing, and so these kinds of situations were to be expected.

"Any word yet on weapons?" John asked.

Peter didn't look hopeful. "So far it isn't looking good. Those who have them don't want to give them up. Some thought we were confiscating their guns. Frank Dawson over by the cul-de-sac, he put up the biggest fuss."

"Idiots," John growled. "Can't they see we're trying to protect them, not take away their Second Amendment rights? I'll head over there after and sort this out."

One of the boys on Peter's side tossed an armful of hockey sticks onto the ground. For a moment John wondered if they intended using them as clubs. Then he made the connection. The sticks were vaguely in the

93

shape of a rifle and could be useful as a temporary substitute for drilling the recruits.

Before he got to that point, John began to lay out his plan. "Our security will consist of two shifts of seven people each. Two at each barricade, two on a randomized patrol around the neighborhood and the final deputy perched in a crow's nest with a view of both barricades. Just like in a sub, it'll be six hours on, six hours off. I suggest in your off-time you practice your rifle skills— cleaning, magazine changes and so on. If you fail to show up for a designated shift you will be punished."

Their faces blanched.

"The recruit in the crow's nest will be given a fog horn to raise the alarm should we come under attack. An approach or assault against the eastern barricade will be signaled by a single blast from the fog horn. Likewise, a threat or assault against the western barricade that protects access from the park will be met by two short blasts. A general breach of the compound will be indicated by three short blasts. I'll spread the word to each of the other committee members so they can inform those under them. If someone approaches the barricades you give them an order to stop and identify themselves. If they keep coming you fire a warning shot. If that still doesn't do it, you open fire."

The new recruits seemed horrified, although some tried not to show it. These were regular facts of life in many countries and war zones, but not here in America. At least not since the Civil War.

John reached into a cardboard box behind him and produced a red dress. Below that was a pair of scissors. The recruits and even Peter looked at him quizzically. He began cutting the dress in long thin strips, knowing all the while that when Diane found out what he had done to her favorite piece of clothing she'd let him have an earful.

Once John finished with the long strips, he cut those into shorter pieces measuring around two feet each. After that he handed them out to each of the recruits and instructed them to tie them around their heads.

"I feel like Rambo," one of the teenage boys said through a nervous giggle.

"Telling friend from foe may be tricky if we come under attack," John told them. "You must prepare yourselves for seeing friends and neighbors you knew coming at you with a gun, intending to take what you have. Reinforcing key points during a battle will be easier if we can see at a glance which of our deputies are already there. There's also something more intimidating about paramilitary forces wearing red headbands that you just don't get with an armband."

The group broke into laughter, John along with them this time, and the release was a welcome one.

Once the cadets were wearing their red headbands, John took them through some basic weapon-handling protocol. It was important that they didn't end up shooting each other by mistake the minute a real gun was in their hands. John picked up one of the hockey sticks and buried the blade into his shoulder with his right foot back and his left foot forward.

"This is how most of you will instinctively hold a rifle for the first time. You've seen Chuck Norris do it. You've seen Arnold and Stallone do it, so it must be right. But in the real world, the bladed-off stance creates two major problems. The first is that you'll experience more recoil when firing. The second is it limits your range of motion when tracking a target." John swiveled back and forth to demonstrate.

"Whether you're shooting a semi-automatic rifle or a pistol, this is the stance you want to assume." John stood with his shoulders squared, feet shoulder-length apart, his right or strong foot staggered six inches behind his left.

"The squared stance will reduce recoil and give you a wider range of motion. Your finger never touches the trigger unless you're ready to shoot." He raised the hockey stick to show them the index finger on his right hand was running along the edge of the blade. "When you do fire, make sure you to squeeze the trigger gently and evenly. You aren't gangbangers from East L.A."

More laughter. The recruits were starting to relax and that was good. John continued with weapon safety tips and shooting drills for the next few hours. He could tell they were getting tired and thirsty working in the hot afternoon sun. He could also see many of them were itching to get their hands on real weapons. John called one of the boys over.

"You're Morton Summers' kid."

"Yes, sir," the boy said. "My name's Alex." Scruffy blond hair and deep blue eyes. This was how Gregory might look in five or six years.

"Alex, go find Susan Wheeler and let her know we need a few two-gallon jugs of water, would you?"

"Yes sir."

Then John went over to Peter. "Do you feel you've been absorbing enough of this?" he asked.

Peter nodded. "Sure, I've done some shooting here and there."

"If I step away for a moment, think you can bring the recruits back through a few more drills?"

"Not a problem," Peter said, smiling. So far, choosing him as second-in-command was the best decision John had made.

•••

A few minutes later, John found Curtis Watkins and Al addressing a small group of older folks. This would be the future diplomatic corps and news branch of Willow Creek. The thought was almost comical. Not by the looks of the team they'd assembled, but because it had become important to do so in the first place.

"Where can I find Frank Dawson?" John asked the two men.

Curtis scratched his chin. "Good question. I remember seeing him over by Patty's place before. He didn't seem in a good mood though."

"That's not a surprise," John replied with a wry grin.

"Good luck," Al offered.

It was another few minutes before John finally found Frank. Turned out he wasn't in Patty's water treatment group at all. He was with Arnold Payne in food management.

"I need to have a word with Frank for a moment if that's all right," John said to Arnold.

"Of course," Arnold said, a clipboard and pen in his hands. "Take the time you need."

Frank didn't look like he had any interest in talking to John. He wore beige cargo pants, the pockets bulging with God knew what. On his right thigh was a tactical holster with what looked like a Beretta 9mm. He rose reluctantly and followed John a few feet away so they could talk.

"I know what this is about," Frank said. His salt-and-pepper hair was neatly combed except for a wave at the back that seemed to be defying orders.

"You haven't locked yourself away in your home, away from all the preparations underway," John said. "That means you care about what's happening, the threat we're facing."

97

"Why shouldn't I? Appleby was a friend of mine and I'm not gonna let them do it to me or my wife."

"I couldn't agree more. And for exactly that reason, I've already allowed the community usage of some of the weapons I own. Most of them were sitting in the basement, locked in a safe not doing anyone a whole lot of good. Can't say I see the logic in letting them rot."

"Yeah, well, Peter already came around trying to convince me to hand them over and I told him where he could stick it."

John laughed. "I'm sure you did. Well, first of all, I think you're in the wrong group. You obviously know your way around firearms. I could use a man like you in security. Unless you prefer taking inventory lists of people's pantries, that is."

A flash of dissatisfaction showed on Frank's face. "Can't say I'm particularly fond of the idea."

"Did you serve?" John asked pointedly.

"Nah. Wanted to, but got a curvature of my spine that always kept me out of the services. Tried three times, even spent six months seeing one of those chiropractors, but in the end they didn't want me."

"I think they made a mistake."

"Reckon you're right about that."

"Why don't you come with me and see what we're up to over in security. Maybe join us in a few drills. No strings attached. If you don't like it better, you can come back to counting cans."

The corner of Frank's mouth curled into a smile. "Why not. Never did like snooping through other people's things anyway."

Chapter 19

Day four came and there was still no sign of Brandon or his family, nor had there been any word from would-be kidnappers. Some sort of ransom note would have arrived by now if foul play had been involved. But in spite of that John was starting to feel a touch of optimism.

He and Peter had managed to procure a half-dozen pistols in addition to the ones John had already donated—a .22 Ruger Mk1, three 9mms and a Heckler & Koch HK45 from John's personal collection. In addition, they also managed to scrounge up a wider variety of rifles. Most of them were deer rifles: Remington 798, Browning T-Bolt, Weatherby Vanguard to name but a few. In the mix were the two Mini-14s and the Bushmaster AR-15 John had given up. He kept his own Colt AR-15 mounted with a Trijicon ACOG Scope on him at all times now, attached to a two-point sling. On his chest he wore an MCR1 Condor Tactical Vest. Housing his S&W M&P40 Pro was a Blackhawk Serpa drop-leg holster. He liked the latter since he would select the angle of his secondary, allowing him to pull it in one quick motion.

The recruits were coming along nicely too. Target practice in the park past the cul-de-sac had sent some of the neighbors scurrying for safety, but the truth was, he didn't want them facing any kind of enemy intrusion without ever having fired a shot before. Ammo wasn't in plentiful supply though, so each of the cadets was only allowed a handful of shots to become proficient. The truth was, they would need to head down to Gold N Guns soon, perhaps today, and see what they could get their hands on.

Frank had become a welcome asset to their security force. Although he was a little rough around the edges, his love of weapons shone through whenever he helped drill the recruits during target practice.

John had hoped the time he'd spent bonding with the Willow Creek defense force might soften his resolve to keep all his guns to himself. If an attack was coming, fending off a well-armed group with deer rifles just wouldn't do.

John had insisted that Diane and the kids sleep in the pod at night. He on the other hand took a couch in the basement in front of the TV. Many a night in the past he'd spent dozing off to a late-night show, the room flickering with diffused light. But now the only things that chased away the darkness were the Coleman lamps that had been part of his prepper kit.

On the day John had assembled his deputies, Gregory had asked him if he could join. It was a question John had known would come sooner or later. He'd taken his son out shooting often and in many ways the kid was perhaps more proficient than some of the recruits, but the thought of putting a twelve-year-old boy behind a barricade with a rifle didn't sit well with him. Had nothing to do with the fact that Gregory was his son. He'd told Peter to search out candidates seventeen years and above. If that minimum age was good enough for the United States military, it was good enough for him. Nevertheless, if a situation ever arose where they needed

100

every hand on deck, Gregory would be able to handle himself just fine.

John was heading for the park when Peter intercepted him.

"I've got some deputies digging a foxhole on Bill Kelsaw's front lawn. We'll reinforce it with sandbags in case the perimeter is breached."

"Excellent," John said.

"Oh, and there's something else. The rest of the security detail is almost done with the watchtower," Peter said, throwing a thumb over his shoulder. The old maple tree on Rose Myers' front lawn had proven an ideal location. Willow Creek Drive ascended slightly as one made their way from Pine Grove east toward the park. A tree stand in Rose's maple would be able to keep an eye on both approaches as well as the surrounding area. That the tree was older and had fewer leaves was an added bonus to visibility.

The bad news was that Rose's back deck had been partially torn apart in order to provide the wood. The lack of power tools had also presented problems. At least half of John's recruits had been sawing two-by-fours all morning to create the platform as well as the ladder which led to it.

A harness would also be added and tied around the tree, providing the person standing watch an added level of safety.

"What do you think?" Peter asked.

John smiled. "It looks great." One of the recruits was already climbing the ladder. The tree stand itself wrapped around the entire trunk. The recruit accessed the platform by emerging through a square cut in the base. It was almost like a treehouse without walls. A wooden railing provided a shooting rest. The recruit walked a full circle around the stand.

"How's the visibility?" John asked.

They threw him a thumbs up.

"There's something else you should know," Peter said. "A black pickup truck, late 70s model, drove past the western barricade twice today. Once in the morning and once in the afternoon."

"How fast were they going?"

"Not fast at all," Peter said.

"If they didn't stop to say hi and reach out," John said, "then I'd be willing to bet they were up to no good."

"There's more."

"Go on."

"Curtis and his fact-gatherers went out into the various neighborhoods of Lakemoor Hills and told us houses have been getting hit all over."

"They went out without an escort?"

"Apparently."

John sighed. "Some of these people still don't fully realize what's going on. They think they can't be hurt, that the law somehow protects them. A human life is cheaper than a can of beans, that's what they don't get."

"I'll talk to Curtis," Peter said, trying to cool John down.

"No, I'll do it at the next committee meeting. Just get one of our deputies with a scoped rifle in that tree stand and make sure they have a fog horn in case there's trouble."

"Will do."

John headed for the barricade at the corner of Willow Creek and Pine Grove. The slightly downward slope was another advantage for defending the street since attackers on foot would be on lower ground. In addition to blocking the street, the barricade now stretched across the lawns on both sides. Two-by-fours with nine-inch nails were placed a few feet back from the wall to puncture the tires of any cars or trucks that tried to ram through.

Frank and one of the older recruits, a man named Mavis, were discussing the difference in range between the average pistol and a deer rifle. Of course Frank wasn't using a deer rifle. He had something from his personal collection. A Heckler & Koch G36 with a telescopic sight, a collapsible stock and a hundred-round drum magazine.

"You're practically a one-man army," John said, trying to clear his mind of the news about Curtis' foolish adventure this morning.

Frank smiled proudly. "Anyone dumb enough to mess with us'll get what he deserves."

"Just remember when you're turning the bad guys into Swiss cheese that those houses over there might be filled with innocent people." John paused. "Listen, I want you two to keep an eye out for a black pickup Peter said was trolling through the neighborhood. If you see it, send word back to me straight away."

"Will do," Frank said. John was about to turn and leave when Frank called after him. "I know now's not a great time, but there's something I wanna show you."

"How long will it take?" John asked.

"Not more than ten minutes or so."

"Okay, come with me." To the recruit he said. "Hang tight, I'll send someone to replace Frank while he's gone."

"Yes, sir."

•••

Not long after they were in Frank's unfinished basement. He reached into the right pocket of his cargo pants and fished out a set of keys. After undoing the

103

latch, he swung the door open. The light from the Coleman lantern threw distorted shadows against the wall. But it was clear enough what Frank had wanted to show John. Hanging from mounts were the closest thing Frank had to children. Pistols, shotguns, semi-automatic rifles and boxes of ammo.

"I got most of the ammo when it looked like the president was gonna take it all away," Frank started. "Did you know that the Department of Homeland Security purchased one point six billion rounds of ammo?"

"Yeah, I read something about that," John said, wondering how much of that load had ended up in Frank's basement.

"I'm not giving most of these out. They're collectibles and incredibly expensive."

"Anything you can spare will be greatly appreciated."

Against one wall were five AR-15's with different configurations. On a work bench were two nightvision goggles. Beside it was a Barrett M107 .50 caliber sniper rifle.

"So let's talk shop, Frank. I won't lie. There's a lot of firepower here. Enough that we wouldn't need to take a risk in hitting that gun shop."

"There won't be nothing left there, believe me. That's the first place most people went. Why waste your time getting food when you can get weapons to take it from someone else? Might makes right."

"You raise a good argument."

"I just wish I knew you were into that prepping stuff earlier," Frank said. "We coulda pooled our resources."

John couldn't help but laugh. "That would have defeated the whole purpose of keeping things on the down low, if you know what I mean. But I've already emptied most of my gun safe for the greater good. I'm just glad you finally saw the light. The collector stuff you can keep, but chest rigs, nightvision, those AR's on the wall and that Barrett—those are things we could really use."

"Only I use the Barrett," Frank said. "That's my only condition. What do ya say?"

John smiled. "How do you feel about heights?"

Chapter 20

Evening came and with it gunfire. John was in the house with Diane and the kids when the sounds stopped them dead. They'd been preparing dinner using the Heartland Wood Cookstove, warming stew that had once been frozen, but that Diane had canned after the deep freeze lost power. The spoon was nearly in John's mouth when he jumped up and headed for the front door.

He hadn't heard the fog horn go off, which meant the shots were either far away or Willow Creek had already been overrun. The S&W was always with him now, along with the AR-15. John peeked out the windows beside the front door before opening it.

Gregory was right behind him.

"Son, you can't come with me. Stay here and keep an eye on your mother and sister, would you?"

The disappointment on Gregory's face was tangible. He wanted nothing more than to follow his father into danger.

"Get the Ruger out of the pod downstairs. There's a box of shells beside it."

"Okay, Dad."

John raced across his lawn, catching frightened faces staring back at him from darkened houses. More loud gunfire echoed as he reached the barricade near Pine Grove. Two recruits were there, one down low out of sight, the other peering out with the nightvision goggles John had equipped them with earlier.

"See anything?" John asked.

"No, sir. I heard screaming before. Sounded like a woman."

"Oh, God help them. Stay alert."

"Will do."

He made his way east, toward the tree stand. With some effort, John climbed the wooden ladder until he reached the platform. Frank was there, peering through the nightvision scope mounted on the rail of his Barrett M107.

"I'm guessing if you'd seen anything, you would have sounded the horn."

"Damn right," Frank said. "There's some kind of battle going on. If you ask me it's coming from a few streets over. Say Taliluna, although it could be as far south as Cherokee Boulevard."

John moved to the south side of the tree stand and peered off in that direction. The stand itself wasn't taller than Rose's house and for good reason. They didn't want to become a target for any crackerjack with a scoped rifle. The flip side was that it made seeing anything outside of Willow Creek Drive nearly impossible. More gunfire now and John caught flashes lighting up nearby houses.

"That's definitely getting closer. Looks like Glenfield Street."

"You might be right. Think it's got something to do with that black pickup we saw skulking around today?" Frank asked.

John kept staring. "It might. Wouldn't want to jump to any conclusions though. We need to be ready in case all this is an elaborate attempt to distract us from something else."

"Like an attack?"

"Maybe. They've driven by and seen how we're set up. It wouldn't take a genius to figure on hitting us where we least expect it."

"Through our backyards."

"Exactly. If I was them, I'd hop a fence and take out the defenders from behind. That's why we need you to keep an eye out on our flanks as well. Let the people at the barricades worry about a frontal assault. I'll send another deputy up to help out." John started climbing down the ladder. "And keep that horn handy."

"Hold up, John," Frank shouted after him. "I got something here you should see."

John climbed back up and followed the tip of Frank's finger. The sight tightened his gut into knots at once. Something was on fire. Looked from here like a house. And without firemen to put it out, who knew how far it would spread. Now there was a new terrifying threat to keep them up at night.

The gunfire wasn't stopping and neither was the shouting. It was low at first, but now it was getting louder. John wanted to block his ears. The cries. The sound reminded him of Kosovo and the ethnic cleansing he'd seen there when his unit had been sent to secure the elections in that shattered country.

"Sounds like a slaughter," Frank said. "Maybe we should go help."

"Help who?"

"Not sure."

"That's the problem," John said. "I know it's hard to hear something like this, but charging in guns blazing when we don't know what the situation is will usually lead to lots of innocent casualties. If you're lucky you kill bad guys, but we're just as likely to kill people on the wrong side."

Frank grew quiet.

108

"Stay focused and keep an eye on that fire if you can, especially if it begins spreading this way."

John climbed down and made his way to the second barricade by the park. The other recruits had since scrambled from their houses. The base of the tree stand was the assembly point if no other sign of danger was visible and Peter addressed them there. It appeared he was ordering them to fan out and watch the perimeter.

Given the volume of fire John was hearing, he couldn't help but wonder if they had enough deputies. Perhaps everyone should have a gun and be trained how to use it? On the surface it sounded like a no-brainer, but it also created a whole other set of issues. You needed lots of bullets for a shooter to become proficient. Bullets they didn't have. It also meant an increase in the chances of friendly fire. Lots of half-trained people running around with guns in the dark was an accident waiting to happen.

The two recruits manning the eastern barricade looked scared to death. They hadn't seen the elephant yet. That was the way soldiers during the Civil War had described facing battle for the first time. Those were the moments where you found out what the man next to you was really made of. Sometimes the biggest, meanest-looking guy with the craziest tattoos went all to pieces at the first sign of gunfire. More often than not, it was the unassuming, wiry guy on your left who kept his emotions in check and carried out his mission.

It was difficult for anyone to trade a soft cushy life for a muddy trench. That wasn't a surprise. For John, the biggest shock was that he'd stayed behind and jumped into the trench along with them.

Chapter 21

John came awake with a start. Weak light trailing in through his living-room windows said it was five, maybe six in the morning. If that were true, it meant he hadn't slept more than a couple of hours. The gunshots had stopped not long before he'd gone to grab some much-needed shuteye, half expecting to be woken from a dead sleep by a blaring fog horn. The alarm hadn't come.

The nerve-wracking events from last night were still playing in John's mind as he stepped into his boots and left the house. The second security detail was on shift. Frank must have also left to rest, since one of the recruits was up in the tree stand. John climbed the ladder and when he reached the top greeted the recruit. They were using a deer rifle. On the platform was Frank's Barrett M107.

"He doesn't want any of us using it," the recruit said.

"Maybe that's for the better. Takes some real training to use a beast like that." John surveyed both barricades. "Anything to report since I left?"

"No, sir. Those fires have died down."

John went to the south end of the platform and scanned the area just past the line of roofs on Willow Creek. Thin black smoke continued to rise, which meant the embers were still smoldering, but the worst of the fire was over. He guessed two, maybe three houses on

Midland Street had completely burned to the ground. He would wait a few hours and make sure there wasn't a resumption of gunfire before sending out a team of three recruits to investigate.

The recruit next to him called him over and pointed toward the Pine Grove barricade. At first all John saw was a man struggling with a large suitcase, walking in the middle of the street. He was heading north, ignoring the barricade as if he didn't see it.

"The man's in shock," John said. He'd seen civilians acting in a similar fashion after their neighborhoods were torn apart by war.

"Where do you think he's going?"

"The interstate," John replied. "That's my best guess." The highways were likely still being used to enter or escape the city by people on foot or on bikes.

Then more stragglers began to emerge and the fog horn sounded with a single, sharp blast. At first they came in pockets of ones and twos, then parents and children and before long groups of families. Some were pushing wheelbarrows filled with personal possessions. Others had shopping carts and anything else they could find to transport their few remaining valuables. John looked on in horror. The sight reminded him of French peasants fleeing Paris as the Nazis approached.

One group cut off from the rest and began heading for the barricade. That was when John climbed down, double-timing it toward Pine Grove. The two recruits manning that checkpoint were speaking with them, but John was too far away to hear what was being said. He arrived a moment later.

"They want to come in," the recruit said, a young girl in her early twenties.

Already more people from neighboring streets peeled away from Pine Grove and headed for the barricade.

"Please let us in. We've been hiding all night. Our street's covered in dead bodies."

"Who attacked you?" John asked, trying not to let his emotions get the better of him.

A middle-aged woman in torn jeans and a dirty sweatshirt had her hands on the sheet metal which formed the front of the barricade wall. "I have no idea, mister. They were shooting anyone who moved, kicking down doors. For all I know, they might have been the police." She put her hands to her face. "It was horrible."

Now other voices were joining hers. Men, women, children crying. Soon there were dozens of people pressed up against the barricade, begging to get in.

"They're gonna come back and kill us all," one man said, tears streaming down his face as he tried boosting his young daughter over the wall. The sight was overwhelming. At the same time, John had to keep his cool just in case this was some kind of diversionary tactic intended to distract them from the main assault force.

John turned back, locked eyes with the recruit in the tree stand and pointed two fingers at his own eyes. He was sending him the message to keep an eye out and stay alert.

The earlier fog horn blast had brought several residents of Willow Creek running from their homes, many of them wielding pistols, shotguns and in many cases kitchen knives, hammers and rakes. They looked like those angry mobs you saw on television back before all the sets in the country got knocked out. John intercepted them and with Peter's help divided them into two groups. None had drilled with the recruits and so he would use them as auxiliaries to plug holes in the perimeter and keep the crowd back from the barricade. But what they needed most right now was an emergency committee meeting.

112

Chapter 22

They met at Patty Long's house again. Her dining room was large enough to accommodate everyone and it only seemed right to keep all the meetings at the same place.

John took a moment to explain the situation. Already, most assembled had listened to the sound of gunfire throughout most of the night. Most were probably thankful Willow Creek had been spared, but that led directly to the point John was about to make.

He stood with his palms flat on the table. "So far it appears our street is the only one that banded together and erected any kind of defensive posture. There's a good chance that had something to do with us not getting attacked last night."

"Do we have any idea who they are?" Curtis asked. As the one in charge of gathering information, he'd been ordered to stay put after going off without an escort. Al was also in the dog house for the same thing, although once the current crisis passed, they'd have the protection they needed to find out more about what was going on out there.

John nodded. "Armed gangs taking advantage of the breakdown in law and order. Hard to say at this point if they came together after the collapse or represent a criminal organization. Either way, they proved last night that they're ruthless and willing to take a human life to get what they want."

Susan Wheeler cleared her throat. "Do we even know what these bandits are after?"

John shook his head. "Right now, we have very little intel. Assume it's the usual. They want what we have. That goes for food, water, weapons and maybe even people. They want to snatch as much money and valuables as they can so when the lights come back on they'll be set for life. Again, I'm speculating. They may not have clued into the fact that it may be months or years before the country's infrastructure will be back online."

"And what about these refugees?" Al said. "I saw them myself stacked against the barricade. Looks like those images of Saigon before the collapse. I'm assuming the main purpose of this meeting is to see how many we can take in."

"How many?" Arnold Payne spat. He was in charge of food management and the very person John had expected to raise the first objection. "I've started going over the data we collected and it isn't looking good. Collectively, we don't have enough food to last more than two weeks and that's with rationing. We take these people in, we'll be signing a death warrant for everyone on Willow Creek."

Al was nodding in agreement. So too was Susan. Her team was in charge of providing fresh water. The greater their water needs, the harder their jobs would be.

"More people might not be a terrible idea," John told the group. "It means more hands to fetch water, more recruits for security."

"More mouths to feed," Arnold chanted.

"There may be ways to produce food," John said.

114

"Does it involve eating squirrels?" Arnold offered with a heavy dose of sarcasm.

John shrugged the comment off. "Not at all. Each and every one of us has a lawn that isn't doing a whole lot. If we strip away the grass, we can use that soil to grow crops. Potatoes, carrots, maybe even corn."

Arnold burst out laughing. "It's not a bad idea, John, but who's going to strip all that grass away?"

"And the water demands will go through the roof. My team is stretched just making sure we have clean drinking water."

John sighed. "No one ever said a life without electricity was going to be easy. Sure, it'll mean lots of work on everyone's part, but how can we just turn them away like animals?"

"I agree with John," Patty Long said. Her medical team had already set up a makeshift treatment center in her house. "I can't imagine condemning people to die."

"We aren't condemning anyone," Arnold shot back. "We aren't the ones who shot up their street last night. The simple truth is, if we start taking in everyone who wants to get in now, where do we draw the line? You wanna talk about playing God, then all the more reason we can't start picking people out of the crowd."

As much as John hated to admit it, Arnold was making a valid point. If they knew these were the only refugees who'd come knocking, the decision might be a manageable one. But who knew what the future would bring?

"I say we take a vote," Arnold said. "All in favor of turning the refugees away raise your hand."

Arnold, Susan and Curtis raised their hands. John and Patty were the only ones who voted no. Al was the solitary vote left and there was a guilty look in his eye as his hand rose and then stopped in mid-air. A third vote for no meant there would be a tie and perhaps room for more discussion. These were people's lives they were debating after all, not what color shirt to wear or whether Bud Light was really less great-tasting.

Finally Al's hand went up and it was settled. Through every stage of his preps John had been comfortable with sacrificing the lives of others in order to save the ones he loved. But seeing it all play out for real, the pain and terror and misery, those decisions he'd thought would be simple were proving to be the most gut-wrenching of all.

Chapter 23

John was the one who would have to deliver the news. He returned to the western barricade near Pine Grove to find that a number of Willow Creek residents had gathered with horror on their faces. This was a scene one would expect to see on the nightly news in a Third World country. Not the USA.

His son Gregory was in the crowd, along with Diane. John felt ashamed of what he was about to do. There was a chair near the barricade the deputies sometimes used during their long watches and John stood on it. There must have been two hundred people pushing up against the barricade, begging to be let in. Recruits were all along the wall, weapons in hand. The one thing they didn't have was a megaphone. It hadn't been part of John's preps since he'd never imagined needing one. He cupped his hands around his mouth so his voice would carry.

"I know all of you are frightened and desperate to get to safety. Our committee's spent the last hour trying to figure out whether we would be able to take any of you in. As it is, our own food stocks are dangerously low. After a difficult vote we've decided we can't take any refugees. I'm sorry."

"What does that mean?" a woman with blood on her face demanded. "If we stay out here we may die."

"You can go and fortify your homes against attack," John offered. "Just like we did."

They didn't seem convinced. "They're burning people's houses, can't you see that? We need weapons. There's safety in numbers."

"I'm sorry," John said. "We took a vote and there's nothing more I can do. I wish you all good luck." The crowd was growing restless. "I need you all to move away from our barricade."

People on the other side were crying, a few of the men cursing at John, telling him their families were going to die because of him. Tears rolled down Diane's cheeks. The enormity of what was happening coupled with the strain on her husband's face must have been too much.

Gregory climbed up on the chair to see, holding onto his dad's waist.

"Son, you shouldn't be up here," John told him.

A boy from the crowd with a red ball cap waved at them and Gregory waved back.

"You know him?"

"Yeah, that's Sean. He's on my baseball team. Can't we just let him and his family in?"

John shook his head. "And what about the rest of them, son? How can we justify allowing some while turning away others?"

"'Cause we know him," Gregory said innocently.

"Don't you think we know most of these people? I see them when I go to the grocery store. I talk to them at your baseball games. See them in the park on the weekends."

Gregory grew quiet and gave a final wave again to his friend in the red cap.

Some of the crowd began moving away as John had instructed and already small groups were walking up Pine Grove, dragging their belongings behind them. But another group of around thirty people weren't leaving. A handful even started pushing against the barricade.

John ordered them to stop, but they weren't listening. If they managed to breach the wall then everyone who had walked away would turn back and flood inside. In other words, all hell would break loose and the lives of everyone would be in danger.

The mob was still shouting and pushing against the wall. John removed his S&W M&P40 Pro and fired three shots into the air. The crowd ducked and then scattered. Within minutes they were all gone. The ground beyond the wall looked like a battlefield, except instead of bodies it was cluttered with the discarded possessions of those who had fled. Maybe they would return to collect them after dark, but either way, someone would take what was there.

It had taken hundreds of years to make a country the greatest on earth and only seconds to turn it into a nation of scavengers.

•••

The last remnants of the mob hadn't disappeared from view for more than ten minutes before shots rang out. Semi-automatic gunfire similar to what they'd heard the night before. The crowd had been heading toward the interstate and it was starting to sound to John like they'd been ambushed.

"We've got to go help them," John said, eyeing the deputies around him. There were seven, surely enough to head out and fend off the attackers. "We can go through Tim Sheridan's backyard." Tim's high wood fence had a gate they sometimes used to enter and exit the perimeter.

John waved them over.

"I don't think this is such a good idea," Peter said. "I mean, what if you all get killed? We can't afford to lose anyone."

"We weren't able to save these people by taking them in. The committee voted and I respect their decision, but I'm sure as hell not going to stand by and listen to them get massacred."

Peter took his arm. "And who'll protect your family and the community when you're dead?"

Shots continued to echo down the street and John double-timed it toward Tim's place, followed by seven deputies. Four of them had AR-15's. Two had deer rifles and one had a Glock 19 from Frank's collection. John had his own AR and the S&W he'd used to disperse the crowd.

Tim's yard had a side gate facing Willow Creek. They entered through there and headed straight for the door facing Pine Grove. John opened the door slightly and didn't see any immediate threats. They moved out onto the street, staying close to the houses for cover, maintaining at least twelve inches from the wall to avoid ricochets and rabbit rounds. Each man guarded a different sector to ensure all angles were covered. They'd drilled several times moving through an exposed area. The firing had died down to little more than sporadic pops here and there.

Pine Grove made a gentle curve to the right as it led up toward the interstate. As John and his seven recruits rounded the turn they saw the bodies. Dozens of them lying on the ground. There was no sign of the gunmen who had done this, nor any of the survivors who'd made it through. Even from far away, one of the dead stood out to John. A kid around Gregory's age, wearing a red baseball cap.

Chapter 24

The massacre on Pine Grove was still soundly on John's mind the following day. Emma had joined the food management team and was busy removing the top layer of grass on Arnold Payne's lawn. It seemed like the perfect opportunity to lend a hand and do what he could to stop seeing the dead bodies every time his eyes closed.

Initially, Arnold had spoken of planting tomatoes and vegetables before John offered a suggestion he thought made more sense. Vegetables or annuals would need to be replanted every year. A more sustainable solution was to concentrate on perennials, plants that would grow year after year without requiring new seeds. The trick was to mimic Mother Nature and plant in concentric circles. Typically, fruit trees provided cover for plants like rhubarb that sought shade. Outside of that shrubs like blueberry and blackberry could grow and beyond that herbs that would act as a screen against pesky insects that might otherwise attack the fruit trees. The added bonus was that the ground around herbs created nitrogen—a natural fertilizer—which the other plants could use to grow.

Other lawns would later be prepped for crops such as corn whenever they managed to find the seeds. John had a stockpile of seeds stored up at the cabin, but he wasn't willing to risk the dangerous trek all the way there to retrieve them.

Food was Arnold's area and John was careful not to overstep his bounds. By now everyone knew very well about the massacre. Tears were spilt, but no one who had voted against taking in the refugees ever admitted they'd sent those people to their deaths.

After his conversation with Arnold, John went back to helping Emma and the others who were prepping the soil for planting. She'd been quiet and withdrawn since Brandon disappeared. So much had changed for all of them in such a short amount of time that there was bound to be an adjustment period. Course, it was one thing to get yourself accustomed to living in a world that had no electricity, hot showers, microwaves, cell phones or iPods. It was another thing entirely getting used to being without someone you cared deeply for.

Emma turned to John. "How long will we have to do this?" she asked.

"I don't know," he replied, using the tip of his spade to separate grass from soil. "I'm hoping the army or National Guard will roll in and let us know what happened, that they're slowly restoring order."

"Do you think the ones who killed those people are gonna come after us next?" she asked, still churning the ground at her feet. She didn't want to look at him, maybe so he wouldn't see the fear in her face.

"Not if I can help it, honey." He'd come to perform a menial task to get his mind off of death and roving gangs and now he was right back where he started.

"Maybe we should just leave and head for the cabin," she said.

John moved in close to her and whispered: "The cabin is a secret, honey. That isn't something we talk about. We've already been over this many times. There

122

isn't any point making preps if everyone in the neighborhood knows about them."

The guilty look that crept over her face made him wonder if she was about to burst into tears. John pulled her into a hug. "I'm sorry, Emma. I'm not trying to make you feel bad. I don't think anyone heard. Besides, they don't know where the cabin is. I just don't wanna do anything that might further jeopardize our safety."

She nodded and wiped her tears away.

A single blast from the fog horn startled them. John's eyes went immediately to the eastern barricade. Both deputies there had their rifles pointed at a man standing with his arms in the air in the middle of Pine Grove. Flapping from one of his raised hands was a white handkerchief.

Chapter 25

John turned. Frank was in the tree stand, lining up the Barrett's crosshairs on the man beyond the barricade. John reached the Pine Grove defenses within thirty seconds. The sound of the horn had brought the entire street to a standstill. After the refugees who'd been slaughtered, the fear spreading through the neighborhood was almost electric.

Peter was at the barricade when John arrived, slightly winded, his heart pounding in his chest.

Is this another refugee? he wondered. *Or someone far worse?*

"Has he said anything?" John asked.

Peter shook his head. "Not yet. He's just been standing in the middle of Pine Grove waving that hanky."

"He's waiting till we tell him it's safe to approach." John climbed up on the chair and took a good look at the man. He wore baggy jeans and a loose-fitting shirt. Every visible inch of his arms was covered in intricate tattoos. But these didn't look like the type that cost hundreds of dollars. These ones looked smudged and poorly drawn. The sort of tattoos men got in prison. A quick look at his face confirmed John's hunch. Long red hair tied into a pony tail. A similar-looking goatee also tied off with an elastic. But what sent shivers up John's arms was the skull tattoo on half the man's face. The other half was clean, but the impression it created was a disturbing one. This guy was unstable. Had a temper. Could snap at any time and commit unspeakable acts.

Maybe the slaughter you saw down the street?

The man's head was tilted slightly to one side as he waved the white handkerchief. He looked like he was possessed, although maybe that was what he wanted John to think.

"What do we do?" Peter asked.

"We see what he wants," John told him, waving the man forward and removing the S&W from his drop-leg holster. The pistol he kept out of view, but at the ready in the event trouble started. When a man with a skull tattooed on his face wanted to talk, it was best to have a gun handy.

The man sauntered forward with an arrogance that worried John. Only two types of people showed that sort of demeanor in a grid-down scenario: the insane and the bad guys.

The man came within ten feet of the barricade when John told him to stop. He tucked the hanky into his back pocket. His fingernails were long, and it made John think of acoustic guitar players.

"Pleasure meeting you fine folks," he said and then glanced up at the sky. A swath of dark clouds were rolling in from the south. "Looks like rain's coming."

"What's your business here?" John asked.

The man's eyes settled on John. "Protection, friend. That's my business. The name's Cain. And you?"

"John."

"Are you the leader here, John?"

"One of them."

"Good, because I have an offer for you. One I'm sure you won't wanna pass up."

"Go on," John said. "I'm listening."

"The world's become such a dangerous place since the pulse bomb hit."

"Excuse me? What pulse bomb?"

Cain grinned as if the idea of everything going bust turned him on. "I call it a pulse bomb, but you're right. There is another name for it. EMP, I believe. Those North Koreans finally did us a favor and fired a nuke into the atmosphere above Kansas City. Knocked out the whole damn grid, man. Melted every computer chip on the continent. Practically sent us back to the Stone Age."

Whether Cain should be believed or not, this was precisely what John had suspected. During the Cold War, both sides had relied on the concept of mutually assured destruction (M.A.D.) to prevent nuclear war. In destroying us, you'd be guaranteeing your own demise. When the Cold War passed, the concept of M.A.D. took a slightly different form. Countries like China and the USA were now linked by strong economic chains. If the economy of one country plummeted, it would bring the others down with it. Mess with us and you risked sinking your own ship in the process.

But now something rather ironic had occurred. The very chains that discouraged our largest enemies from attacking us only emboldened our smallest enemies. Detonating an EMP over America would at once sink the biggest economic power in the world and drag down everyone else with her. A perfect strategy that only a country like Iran or in this case North Korea could fully benefit from.

John swallowed hard. "How do you know this?"

"Some of the men in our… group… are former military. They tell me things may be down for months. Maybe longer. Which is why we're here, to offer you and your people protection. In exchange for a small price, we can guarantee no one touches you. All we ask is a

126

monthly donation of food and water. Say thirty percent of whatever you collect."

"We don't need protection," John shot back.

"Everyone needs protection, friend." Cain was grinning again, but only on half of his face.

"Besides," John went on, "we don't have enough food or water to spare. That's why we were forced to turn away those refugees."

"Yes, I saw you chase them off. Whatever became of them?" Cain asked.

"I'm sure you know perfectly well."

"Believe me when I tell you thirty percent is a cheap price to pay for your safety."

John gripped the pistol in his hand and Cain's eyes narrowed as though he could see what was in John's mind. "You shoot me and there'll be a hundred men to take my place and none of them are nearly as kind or forgiving."

"Is that all you wanted?" John asked coolly.

"I think it's in your best interest to take our offer seriously. We'll give you until first thing tomorrow. If you agree to our terms, hang a white bedsheet from this barricade. If we come around and there isn't a white sheet, we'll assume you've refused our generous offer."

A black pickup drove into the intersection and Cain nodded, walked over to the truck, and got into the passenger seat before the truck drove away.

Chapter 26

"What do we do?" Al asked, visibly flustered.

The council had assembled in Patty Long's dining room for their third and perhaps most important meeting yet.

"Thirty percent of our food each month," Arnold said. "That's unreasonable. We'll starve to death."

"What did you tell him?" Patty asked, sweeping back her wavy blonde hair.

John rubbed at the tension building at his temples. "I told him we didn't need any protection. Then he suggested we think about it and made reference to the dozens if not hundreds of bodies lying on Pine Grove."

"It's a shakedown," Curtis said. His nose was shaped like a bird's beak and with his wide frantic eyes he was starting to act like one too. "I've read about this kinda stuff. It's a racket."

"There's a very good chance we're dealing with a gang of drug dealers or gangbangers," John said, still picturing the skull tattoo on Cain's face. "Can't say yet how many of them there are, but they seem to be taking a page out of the mafia's handbook. Back in the day, if you opened a restaurant in New York City a guy in a pinstriped suit would pay you a visit and offer you protection insurance. Thousand bucks a month, maybe more. If you said no, the next day your shop was firebombed."

"They killed all those innocent people," Susan said in disgust. "I think we should just give them what they want."

Hearing that made John's temperature spike. She was one of the council members who had voted to send those refugees to their deaths in the first place. Now she was advocating opening a Pandora's box with men who would think nothing of killing them all. "Today they're asking for thirty percent," John said, directing his comments at Susan in particular. "A steep amount of resources by any measure. And what will we do when thirty percent becomes forty percent and then fifty percent? Haven't any of you read your history? The Romans bribed barbarian hordes not to attack the empire and each time the barbarians returned demanding more money."

"What do you propose?" Patty asked.

"If we pay them," John said, "they'll think we're weak and keep taking until we starve to death. If we refuse, we run the risk of an all-out war. A war we may not win."

Al was shaking his head. "So basically you're asking if we prefer starving to death or being shot."

"Not exactly," John replied. "I'm saying that if we pay them, we'll starve to death for sure. If we don't, then there's a chance we could prevail. It'll mean at least doubling the number of deputies."

"I thought you said we were low on guns as it was," Arnold barked.

John nodded. "We are low. Although there's enough now to arm thirty deputies, but many of them won't have much more than pistols. Unfortunately, a few of those will be .22 caliber. But if we present ourselves as a hard

129

enough target, it may encourage these guys to pick on someone else."

"But with so many deputies," Arnold countered, "it'll rob manpower from food production and water purification."

"We can take them from information and liaison," John suggested. "With bandits ravaging Sequoyah Hills, I doubt very much we'll find groups nearby to trade with anyhow."

Al and Curtis didn't seem pleased by the suggestion.

"Don't worry, gentlemen, you'll still have a place within the committee and once the current crisis passes then we can repopulate your teams."

"My big concern is water," Susan said, before John was even completely finished. "We've extracted the water from the pipes of nearly every house on the block. It won't be another day or two before we need to send groups south to the Tennessee River, our only source of water. How on earth will that be possible if armed criminals are threatening us?"

She raised a valid concern. Just like medieval fortresses, maintaining a safe and continuous flow of water was a constant security challenge. "When that time comes," John said, "we can organize armed escorts. Say five or more deputies armed with semi-autos." The thought of offering the use of Betsy occurred to him, but the risk was too great. If he ever lost the Blazer, it would punch a major hole in his ability to bug out once the situation became untenable. "I think it's important to remember we're deciding between a bad option and one that's even worse," John told the committee. "These are bad men. If we stick together and everyone does their jobs, then we might just make it through this."

There was one more thing John needed to tell them. It was the information Cain had given him about the

EMP. Sure, there was no way to know whether Cain was telling the truth, but everything he'd said was in line with the research John had done years before.

"So we were attacked," Arnold said.

John tapped his fingers in a somber rhythm. "Seems that way."

"What does it mean for us then?" Al asked.

"Means the cavalry probably isn't coming any time soon," John told them. "If we're going to get out of this mess, it'll have to be by our own hand."

Al and Curtis were eyeing Patty's dining-room table, lost in the enormity of the situation.

Susan took a deep breath. "All in favor of rejecting Cain's offer of protection raise your hand."

The vote was nearly unanimous. Five hands went up. Only Curtis voted to accept. There would be no white sheet along the barricade as Cain had asked. Either way, the die was cast and the fate of Willow Creek about to be decided.

Chapter 27

There wasn't going to be enough time before Cain's deadline to train all of John's new deputies. There were thirty in all now, not including John and Peter, and as he had told the committee, most of them had little more than a pistol. Their newly swelled ranks amounted to roughly thirty percent of Willow Creek's population. No doubt the increase in defense would put a serious strain on their ability to gather the other necessities for sustaining life.

All through the night the community had been on edge. John had slept little more an hour and even then he'd only tossed and turned on the living-room couch.

Cain had told them yesterday to hang a white bedsheet over the barricade if they intended to accept his offer. No sheet was hung. That part wasn't a surprise. The unknown part was what would happen after. Would Cain and his men storm the barricades and slaughter them all as they had done to the refugees, or would he sit back and wait for the residents of Willow Creek to become complacent and make a mistake?

John spent that morning moving between each of the barricades. He'd also sent spotters onto the roofs of a handful of houses on both sides of the street. The idea was to ensure that intruders—Cain's men or otherwise—didn't cut through a neighbor's fence and breach the perimeter. Tactically, using the roofs had presented its own set of problems, since the men and women up there were prone on the side facing Willow Creek Drive. That meant they were less visible to anyone approaching through the backyards, but were vulnerable to sniper fire from Pine Grove. For that reason, John selected houses with chimneys on the west side of the structure—the side facing Pine Grove—in order to provide them with a degree of cover and protection.

This wasn't your typical urban environment where a soldier was encouraged to blast holes in walls and roofs or knock them down entirely so he could create loopholes to shoot from. Damaging these homes would mean letting rainwater in which led to mold and rot.

Arnold's food management team, although diminished numerically, was out tearing up more grass to make way for crops. Once that part was done, they would gather as much topsoil as they could from the flower gardens of every house on the block. In that department, Al's love of gardening had proven particularly useful since he had a number of unused bags of soil sitting in his garage. Given that his services as liaison officer weren't in high demand at the moment, he was happy to make himself useful.

John had just finished instructing some of the new recruits on gun safety when Diane came up to him. Like everyone else she seemed nervous and spoke in a low voice, as though Cain or one of his men might be eavesdropping.

"How you holding up?" he asked.

"Not nearly as well as I thought I'd be. Any sign of Cain?"

John shook his head. "No, and I don't expect there to be. He's likely set up a spotter in a house within sight of the barricade. He knows perfectly well that if we've refused his offer, we're liable to shoot him if he shows his face."

Diane was wringing her hands and John could see red marks on her palms and fingers from where she'd been kneading out her frayed nerves. "I can't tell you how much I hate this, John. You remember our conversation in the kitchen—if things got out of hand we'd head to our bug-out location. I think maybe it's time we do that now."

"Honey, you were the one who suggested we stay. The pod in the basement was only really intended for short-term emergencies. Ice storms, tornadoes, blackouts. That sorta thing. It was never intended to get us through an EMP attack."

"But at the start," Diane said, "we still weren't certain what we were up against. It made sense to give it a few days. John, you're so close to it all that you may not be able to see clearly, but things are starting to escalate. The situation was dangerous enough staying in a city without power, now we have a gang of thugs who've demonstrated a willingness to kill indiscriminately."

"So what are you saying, Diane? That we just up and leave the people around us at the very moment when they need us the most?"

Her eyes lowered. "I'm frightened, John, and so are the kids."

He took her in his arms, her body quivering as he squeezed her tight. When John looked up, Patty Long came toward him. She was in charge of Willow Creek's health needs and the look on her face wasn't a good omen.

Diane saw Patty and wiped the tears from her eyes. Diane was on her team and she was surely feeling self-conscious breaking down in public.

"I'm guessing the news you have isn't very good," John said.

"Dorothy Klein died last night."

Diane covered her mouth. "Oh, no."

"She was eighty-two years old," Patty said. "But it wasn't her age which did it. She'd run out of Danaparoid for her heart and we didn't have anymore to give her."

"We sent a team out a few days ago," John said. "And they came back empty-handed. Whatever the pharmacies once had, it was long gone by the time we arrived."

"Rose Myers' daughter Summer is diabetic and dangerously low on insulin. We've also got a dozen others with heart and other medical problems, a pregnant woman and lots of cases of what seems to be PTSD, not to mention a child with a fever we haven't been able to break. We need to get some medicine, one way or another."

"Okay," John said. "I'll talk to Peter and see what we can do."

A fresh bout of anxiety washed over Diane's face. She'd been married to John long enough to know he was about to do something dangerous.

Chapter 28

John found Peter near the western barricade, drilling the rest of the new recruits. Before Cain showed up, they would have done so in the park, but now leaving the perimeter defenses was too risky.

To fill the ranks, the security team had had to choose from a pool of slightly older residents. They'd made a special point of not taking anyone younger than seventeen. The last thing they wanted was to employ the same tactics as the rebels in Sierra Leone who filled their ranks with children as young as ten.

"How's it going?" John asked. Peter was teaching them how to leapfrog. The eight recruits were divided into teams of four and given a signal, in this case 'tango'. Team one would provide suppressing fire on the designated target while team two would reposition. When the signal was given, they would switch roles, enabling the troops to advance under relative cover. But it was clear the concept wasn't working very well. When team two repositioned they gave the signal without providing any covering fire.

Peter slapped his forehead. "Stop and get back to your starting positions." He turned to John. "I feel like if it hits the fan, one of these people is gonna shoot me in the back by mistake."

John smiled. "Or they may just save your life."

Peter ordered the recruits to take a knee. John then told him about his conversation with Patty and the need for insulin, heart meds which included Danaparoid, Benazepril and Betaxolol, as well as valium and a long list of others.

"Didn't you tell her we already sent people to a handful of pharmacies and they were cleaned out?"

"I did, but we're gonna start losing people fast, including Rose Myers' ten-year-old daughter, if we don't do something soon."

"You have a place in mind?"

John nodded. "There's a small, family-run pharmacy over on Lakeview. Real itty-bitty thing. My guess is that most of the large chain stores have been hit, but the smaller ones may still be intact."

"You'll have to go on foot," Peter said, concerned. "Otherwise you risk drawing too much attention from those raiders who are trying to extort us."

"I know. My plan is to take four others, including Frank, and be back within an hour or two."

Peter didn't look thrilled with the idea. "You'd be leaving us kinda thin. I mean, we have all these new recruits, but with five of you gone, that leaves us with what, less than ten competent deputies to maintain the perimeter?"

"I know, but I don't see any other way. If the trip was going to take more than a couple hours then I'd agree we could wait. But Cain or his men won't harass us until they're sure we've turned down their offer."

"Maybe," Peter replied. "Either way, I'll keep marching these guys around in a show of force and hope it's enough to keep Cain and his gang of looters at bay."

•••

Twenty minutes later, John, Frank and three deputies slipped out of Willow Creek via the park by the eastern barricade. They needed to be quick and carry back supplies, so travelling light was key. John and Frank were the only ones carrying any serious firepower. Each wore a tactical vest loaded with four thirty-round magazines, their Colt AR-15s attached to a two-point shoulder sling. John's drop holster carried his favorite pistol, while Frank opted for a Glock 21. Even though it was daytime, they were also dressed in camo-pattern pants and shirt, their faces painted black and green. Despite the suburban setting, there was still plenty of shrubs and greenery for them to use as cover.

The deputies were similarly dressed, except one of them carried a Remington deer rifle and the other two SIG P228s.

Sequoyah Hills formed a sort of peninsula that jutted out into the Tennessee River. Lakeview Drive hugged the edge of the river as it wound up toward the interstate and John decided this was the best avenue of approach. They wouldn't walk along the river itself to avoid getting ambushed and pinned against the water's edge. Instead they would make their way north, hugging house to house as they went. The idea was to skirt around whatever forces Cain had in the area and be back before anyone knew they were gone.

After moving from house to house for nearly thirty minutes, they reached the corner of Lakeview and Woodland. That was when John spotted the black pickup rolling slowly through the intersection. He held up his arm, hand in a fist, and the group stopped, dropping for cover. Both he and Frank peered out from behind a burning bush shrub, watching through the scopes of their rifles.

138

The truck was moving very slowly, as though they were looking for someone.

"A patrol?" Frank whispered.

"I hope so," John replied. "I can't imagine they'd be looking for us specifically."

Eventually the pickup moved out of sight and they continued on. The front doors on many of the houses they encountered were ajar, the wood frames splintered from being kicked in. Likely it was Cain's men, scavenging for food and other valuables. None of the houses seemed to be occupied and John was left to wonder where the people had all gone.

Before long they reached Tipton's Pharmacy. It was a small family-run place that had been there for years. Many of the locals continued to buy their prescription drugs from Tipton's for that very reason. In Knoxville a warm smile went a long way.

The front door and window were shattered. It was beginning to look as though they'd come all this way for nothing. As the group approached, a body lying face first over the shattered front window came into view. Blood pooled below a man in jeans and a white sweater. Only the sweater wasn't white anymore, it was splattered with blood and dirt. The lack of a wound on the man's back told John he had likely been killed as he entered the store.

The glare from the sun overhead made it difficult to see inside the darkened store. Glass crunched under their feet as they drew near.

"That's far enough," a voice shouted from inside. It was a man and he sounded old.

"Jeb," John called out. "That you in there?"

"One more step and I'll give you what I gave that looter."

John wasn't more than a few feet from the body now and he could see the dead man was wearing a Memphis

139

Grizzlies sweater. He didn't look a day over thirty. Certainly didn't fit the stereotype of a hardened criminal. More likely he was a family man from the neighborhood, coming to fill a prescription for someone in dire need, much like them.

"We don't want any trouble, Jeb," John told him. "We got some sick people over on Willow Creek Drive and we need some medicine for them. Is Marlene in there with you?"

"My wife is fine, John. I've known you for a number of years now, but I'm telling you that no one's gonna take my stuff by force. Not if I have a say in it."

The truth of the matter was, John hadn't expected the pharmacy to be occupied. The idea of Jeb standing guard with his wife hadn't factored into things.

"We don't intend to take anything, Jeb. Especially by force. Why don't we give you a list of what we need and we'll see if we can make a trade."

Jeb was quiet for a minute. "Go ahead and toss that list in here, John, and I'll have a look."

John did as Jeb asked and backed away. The dead body lying on the shattered window was starting to stink and John was happy to move away from it.

"I think I can get you most of this," Jeb said. "Packed the insulin fridge with some ice when the power went down and it's been keeping real nice."

"That's good, Jeb."

"So what's your offer then?"

John hadn't brought anything to barter with. He had to think fast.

"When's the last time you or Marlene had something to eat, Jeb?"

Jeb was slow to answer. "It's been a while. Neither of us has set foot outside since the lights went out. I ain't gonna let those vultures swoop down and steal all my hard work."

"I don't blame you. Are you hungry?"

"Sure," he said. "But mostly I'm thirsty. Bit ashamed to admit the wife and I've been drinking from the toilet these last few days."

"Give me a minute, Jeb, and I'll see what I can do about that." John moved a few feet away to huddle with Frank and the three deputies. "Give me your canteens," he told the deputies. Reluctantly, they removed them from their belts and handed them over. "What about food? Any of you bring anything to eat?"

Frank opened a pouch on his vest and produced a bag of trail mix. "It isn't much, but it's all I got."

John had water in his CamelBak, but not a stitch of food. This would have to do. They moved back near the broken window. "Jeb, you still there?"

"Course I am. Told you I ain't going nowhere."

"We can offer you three canteens of water—"

"Not good enough," Jeb shot back.

John sighed. "Our street is struggling to get by as it is. What if we made room for you and your wife in our community? We've got barricaded walls and some food, but most of all, protection from roaming gangs. It's only a question of time before they find you."

"How many times do I have to tell you we ain't leaving?"

John felt the hope slipping between his fingers. Cantankerous as he was, Jeb's inventory would have made a nice addition to Patty's store of medical supplies. Just then John remembered something. In a utility pouch were crackers from an MRE he'd opened weeks ago. They were still sealed and hadn't gone bad.

"All right, Jeb. Here's our final offer. Three canteens of purified water, one bag of trail mix and sealed crackers from an MRE."

There was silence for a while after that. Then Jeb spoke. "Still a weak offer, John. But I'll tell you what. You hand all that over and I'll give you your insulin and half of the heart meds you asked for. I ain't giving you any valium or any Danaparoid or Benazepril. You come back with something besides water and crackers and you can have the rest."

John sighed. If he'd known Jeb would be here he might have brought some gold and other tradable items. For now he would take what he could get. "You've got yourself a deal, Jeb."

"Good, now go ahead and toss those things in and I'll get your meds."

"Here they are, Jeb," John said, dangling them in the open slot where the window once stood. "Bring my meds and we'll make a clean swap."

Jeb grumbled. "Fine." There was movement from inside as Jeb shuffled around. At one point it sounded as though he was arguing with someone. The deputies continued to scan the perimeter as Jeb finally returned. This time he came right to the window and handed them a brown paper bag. In turn, John gave him the canteens and the other food. Jeb smiled, looking pale and thinner than usual.

"Wife's in there bitching to high hell. Figured if I showed myself and y'all shot me, you'd be doing me a favor."

John smiled. "The offer still stands to join us."

Jeb shook his head.

"Sad to hear it, Jeb. We'll be back then to get the rest. Keep yourself safe."

"Godspeed," Jeb replied and disappeared back into the inky darkness of the pharmacy.

Chapter 29

John and the others made their way south along Lakeview until they reached Woodland. The expedition so far had been long, tiring and stressful. They would all be glad to get back to the relative safety of Willow Creek.

Huddled behind the corner house, John peered out to ensure that the coast was clear. When he didn't spot any threats he gave the signal for them to move. Crossing over open terrain was one of the most dangerous times for a soldier and John's heart hammered in his chest as all five of them sprinted across Woodland Drive. They were less than halfway there when John heard a noise on their right. Sounded like someone whistling, the sort you might hear at a concert or when someone was hailing a cab.

John scanned right. A spotter on the roof of a nearby house was whistling and pointing in their direction. Then an engine roared to life and tires squealed. The older black pickup tore out of a driveway. The windows were tinted but in the truck bed were two men with automatic rifles.

"Run!" John shouted as he tossed Frank the medicine. Bringing up the rear while the others raced off ahead, John kept an eye out for the pickup which he knew was about to come barreling around the corner onto Lakeview. Running away from a gun battle was a great way to get shot in the back, which was why he would cover his friends' retreat.

When he heard the truck approach, he dropped to the ground behind a group of stone steps and rested his AR into a supported firing position. It had been years since he'd fired a shot in anger, but instinct was quickly settling in. He quieted his breathing as the pickup appeared. The two men in the back fired wildly at Frank and the others. John squeezed the trigger three times in quick succession.

Two of the shots landed low. The third cut through the truck's sidewall. The two men standing in the truck bed banged on the hood and the truck sped east on Woodland. John laid off a handful more shots, forcing the men in back to duck for cover. It seemed as though he'd frightened them away, which was good enough for him.

Frank and the others were three houses ahead of him and John rose and hurried to catch up. Between the tactical vest, full magazines, his AR and sidearm he was having a tough go of it. He made another mental note on his list of things to do: Get in better shape. It was good and fine to have a fully stocked bunker in your basement, but if you couldn't run for your life when the time came, it might all be for nothing.

Behind him came the roar of the truck. He turned briefly to see it rocketing west now on Woodland. The black pickup was going in the opposite direction and John wasn't sure why. He hurried nevertheless, tracking the noise the truck made as it raced through the back streets. Then it dawned on him. They were trying to cut them off before the park, and there was no way to warn Frank.

John charged ahead, shouting Frank's name, but when the adrenaline was running high, your hearing was sometimes the first sense to dull.

The truck's engine roared louder and John expected to see it coming straight for him every time he hit another cross street.

Up ahead was the park. Frank and the deputies were less than two houses away. There was one last street between him and safety. John took a quick look, saw nothing and made a break for it. As he did, shots rang out striking the side of the house he was using as cover. Chunks of brick filled the air. They had him zeroed in. Now he could hear the truck on the move again, but it wasn't coming toward him. It was circling back around. The driver must have dropped off the two in the truck bed and was now coming around so he could approach from the south on Lakeview and catch John in a pincer movement.

Frank and the others were alerted to the situation after hearing the most recent shots and the three of them doubled back. The last deputy kept running through the park and into Willow Creek, presumably to deliver the meds in case none of them made it back alive.

There wasn't a lot of time. From across the street, John used hand signals to let Frank know there were two shooters west of them, moving closer. The deputies took cover in a gully and prepared to engage the pickup when it arrived. At least one of them had the Remington deer rifle, which offset the first man's SIG pistol.

What John really wanted was for Frank to use suppressing fire to pin down the two who were cutting off his escape. That way he could cross the street before the truck showed up.

He threw Frank more hand signals telling him to lay down the suppressing fire he needed. No sooner had he done so than the pickup came skidding onto Lakeview. The passenger window was down and a man hung out the opening with an assault rifle. Without any cover, John

146

did the only thing he could. He dropped to the ground to create the smallest possible target, hoping the move wouldn't force him to lose precious time before he could return fire with his AR. Dirt kicked up around him as rounds from the truck narrowly missed. Both deputies were now shooting as well. One scored a hit through the front windshield and the car swerved, tossing the shooter back and forth. John saw an opportunity and followed suit. If he could kill the driver, the passenger would be a sitting duck. Using the Trijicon ACOG Scope mounted on his AR, he squeezed the trigger a half-dozen times in rapid succession. The truck's windshield fragmented into a giant spiderweb, sending the vehicle swerving onto a nearby lawn.

A second later it crashed into one of the houses. Steam rose from the engine. John put three more shots into the passenger side door, aiming low. He didn't want to kill the man who'd been shooting at him. Not yet at least.

From across the street, Frank shouted that the two shooters had turned and run away when they saw the pickup crash.

The driver was presumably either dead or seriously wounded. That left the passenger alone.

"We've got you covered," John shouted as he cautiously approached. "Throw your weapons out the window and we'll let you live."

He heard the faint sound of a man groaning in pain.

Frank kept an eye on the rear to make sure the other two didn't double back.

A moment later the man in the passenger seat tossed a Chinese Type 56 (AK-47) out the pickup's window. Then another along with two Beretta 9mms.

John approached from the rear the way police officers did during a traffic stop. In that way he could cut

147

the angle in case the guy in the truck decided to try something smart. The two deputies approached from the south, moving along the line of houses, each with weapons at the ready.

When they were both within ten feet John said: "Are you hit?"

"My leg's shot up," came the reply and it was clear he was in serious pain.

"Put your hands out the window where we can see them."

The man complied. He had tattoos etched across the knuckles of his fingers. Put together, the letters spelled out a rather nasty curse word.

The two deputies collected the weapons on the lawn.

John then opened the passenger door and pulled the wounded man out. He fell onto the ground like a sack filled with dirty laundry, yelping in pain. His jeans were bloody from the knee down. Looked like John had placed those final shots well.

Inside the cab, the other man appeared to be dead. John slung his AR over his shoulder, removed his S&W and crawled into the cab to feel for a pulse. There was none. It wasn't clear which of them had been the one to kill the driver, but either way this death wouldn't be the last. If Cain had had any doubts before about his offer, now he would know it had been soundly rejected.

Chapter 30

They took the man prisoner and kept him under armed guard in the Wilsons' empty house. They also took the truck. The collision hadn't done much to harm the engine—nothing that couldn't be fixed. Didn't matter if the fender and grill were dented. Having a truck to fetch water and perform other chores would really help.

Betsy was still in John's garage. He'd been reluctant to bring the Blazer out since it represented his only real means of getting him and his family to safety. Working vehicles were a hot commodity in a country where everyone was suddenly on foot.

The gun battle had rattled many people's nerves on Willow Creek. With a group of their own out on a mission, rumors had begun to spread that they'd all been killed. Peter had even begun organizing a group to head out and see what was going on. But intense as it was, the gun fight hadn't lasted longer than about ten minutes, and by the time Peter was approaching the eastern barricade, flanked by deputies, the action was all over.

The exchange had also shown John that when push came to shove, his deputies had performed better than expected. Of course, the mission wasn't a complete success. They'd gone out with a laundry list of meds to retrieve and come back with less than half of what they needed. That would mean they'd need to make another trip and bring more men along with them when they did.

Diane had been using the pressure canner to sterilize t-shirts for cloth bandages when she heard what was happening and came running to greet the men as they returned. Gregory and Emma were there too along with many of the other residents. The men were greeted as heroes, but the expression on Diane's face was something else entirely. She hadn't wanted him to go out in the first place. Let someone else's husband risk his life.

But that wasn't the kind of man John was. In combat, he never asked his men to do something he wasn't willing to do himself.

Patty Long had also been in the crowd, gawking along with everyone else at the bloodied prisoner they brought back with them. To the gathering crowd, these were the drug dealers who had kidnapped the Applebys and nearly killed the Hectors. A taste for revenge was in the air and John was sure a few among them would love to finish the man off. But John needed him alive, at least for now. Even when Patty told him they should organize another committee meeting to discuss what had happened, John told her it would have to wait. He had some questions of his own he needed answered first.

•••

Not long after, they set up in Dr. Wilson's empty basement. The wounded man's jeans had been cut off at the knee, revealing the extent of his injuries. It seemed a tragedy to use the fresh bandages Diane and Patty Long's medical crew had been making since yesterday, but John hoped the intel would be worth the price.

Patty and her assistant worked for an hour stemming the bleeding and sewing his wounds. The bullets had

150

gone straight through the soft part of the man's calf, which was lucky for him since it meant no broken bones or lead fragments that needed to be removed with tweezers. Painkillers were the one thing John had refused to give him.

Peter and Frank were both there as Patty and the others shuffled out.

The man wore loose baggy clothes similar to how Cain had been dressed. His hair was dark, greasy and hung in his face. A scar ran across his right temple. In spite of his injuries, his arms and legs were bound with paracord.

"What's your name?" John asked, pacing before him.

The man winced with pain. The wound in his leg was clearly starting to throb. "Why should I tell you anything? You're just gonna kill me."

"You'll die for sure if you don't talk," Frank shot from behind them. "That's a promise."

"Your name. What is it?"

"Your mother, that's my name."

John kicked the man's bound legs and the man let out a screech of pain.

"I don't want to hurt you anymore than I already have. Answer our questions and we'll see to it you're treated fairly."

His eyes were welded shut in agony. "James. My name is James."

"Thank you, James," John said cordially. "What's your last name?"

James hesitated. John's eyes dropped to James' legs and the implied threat of another kick seemed to jog his memory.

"Clay. My name's James Clay."

"You're one of Cain's men." John stated it as a matter of fact.

James nodded. "Guess you could say that. I'm part of his crew."

"Crew?"

"Meth. Cain has labs all over the city. Mobile homes, basements, you name it."

"You're drug dealers."

"We're businessmen. We're venture capitalists. We can sniff out an opportunity and that's exactly what Cain saw when the lights all went out. But if you think we're the only ones you're fooling yourself. This whole city's being carved up as we speak. Big fish eating little fish and getting fatter and fatter."

It was sounding to John like Mogadishu, where local warlords effectively controlled the city with an iron fist, keeping its citizens in a perpetual state of fear and panic.

"What does Cain want with us? We haven't done a thing to him."

James snickered. "You're still not getting it. Sequoyah Hills is Cain's turf, his fiefdom. You and everything you own belong to him."

"The hell we do," Peter cried, coming forward.

John and Frank held him back.

"How many men does he have?" John asked after they'd managed to calm Peter down.

"Couple hundred. But more are coming in everyday. Cain has a real knack for making people do what he wants."

There was a scar along James' neck, as though someone had held a knife there and pushed until the blade broke the skin.

"That how he convinced you?"

"Maybe. But that's ancient history. I been working for Cain for almost five years."

"Does he have any other vehicles?"

"Cain gets whatever he wants. You steal one of his trucks, he'll find ten to replace it. You people can't win."

"We'll see about that," John replied. "Where's he headquartered?"

James scoffed. "I ain't telling you that. I'm already dead if he finds out I said a word to you people."

John knelt down and grabbed the meat of James' wounded calf. "I'm gonna ask you one more time."

"I told you—"

Closing his fingers tight, John listened to the man howl in pain. He hated having to resort to such barbaric methods, but when it came to protecting his family and by extension the people of Willow Creek, he was willing to do whatever was needed.

"He's on Towanda Trail. 552 Towanda Trail. Please just stop. Please."

John let go.

"He's over by the interstate," Frank said.

"Makes sense," John replied. "That way he can control the flow of human traffic in and out of Sequoyah Hills. Maybe even raid the highway from time to time and nab survivors to satisfy his perverted pleasures."

John was heading for the door when Peter said: "What do we do with him?" He was pointing at James who was doubled over in pain.

"Keep him here and make sure a deputy's watching him at all times. We may have some more questions for him."

•••

The committee meeting which followed was frantic. The entire community was justifiably frightened and John felt a need to balance telling them the dire truth of their situation with the risk of inciting panic. Luckily, Susan

Wheeler, perhaps the most excitable of the bunch, was off with her team restocking the water supply.

The most important facts were that Cain was a dangerous man and that he meant business.

"He's a local drug dealer who's using his street thugs to claim Sequoyah Hills as his own," John explained.

Al looked positively beside himself. "I'd really hoped he was just bluffing this whole time."

"Where's the National Guard?" Arnold moaned, his mouth locked in an expression of disbelief.

"I'm sorry to say we're on our own here," John told them starkly. "If the Guard or even the army still exists, I'm sure they've got bigger fish to fry. And that's exactly why a lowlife like Cain is taking advantage of the situation. We got four more weapons from his men. Two Chinese AK-47s and two Beretta 9mm pistols. They'll come in handy, but each of us needs to be extra vigilant. I suggest everyone who has a weapon in their home for self-protection keep it on their person at all times." John wasn't done yet. "If we'd taken in those refugees earlier, not only would they still be alive, but we'd have a larger defense force to draw on."

"I hope you're not holding us responsible for the deaths of those people," Curtis exclaimed. "We weren't the ones who pulled the trigger. How were we supposed to know that would happen?"

John wasn't buying it for one second. "Fact are facts. The night before we all heard the gunfire. What did you think was going on? You chose to save yourselves and now we're in a tougher spot because of it."

"You're not being realistic, John," Arnold said. "As it is we're low on food. We would have all starved to death."

Patty clapped her hands together, making the bracelets on her wrists clang together. "And how do we

154

know what chronic medical conditions they were bringing in with them? We already have one young girl with diabetes and we're struggling to keep her going."

"I'm not saying the choice was an easy one," John told them. "What I'm saying is that with a breakdown of law and order, security is always a grave concern. Gangs forming to prey on the weak is a fact of life in every country where the police aren't there to help people. We need to stop thinking that we're any better, or any different."

Just then, Peter burst into the room, startling the committee members. The look on his face spoke volumes and none of it was good.

"What is it?" John asked, his pulse quickening.

"There's been an accident."

Chapter 31

The wounded were being carried in from the park by deputies. Two men and one woman. Their clothes were soaked in blood. A gash across the woman's head was bleeding badly. Diane, Emma and other members of the medical team were there to receive them.

"What happened?" Patty asked, checking their wounds as they came in.

"We were ambushed at the river," the man said. His name was Tray Lynch—he was an insurance salesman who lived in a house by the park. He was on Susan Wheeler's water management team.

"What about the others?" Diane asked.

Susan was nowhere to be seen, along with two men from her group and the two deputies who'd gone with them to provide security.

The crush of residents rushing in was making it hard to get them to safety and John ordered some of his deputies to form a barrier so they could get to Patty's living room which had recently been converted to a triage center.

John followed them in and closed the door behind them. He needed to find out what had happened, who had done this and where Susan and the missing residents and deputies were. In all, Susan normally went to fetch water with five other members of her group. Each of them rode bikes with baby trailer attachments they used to pull the water they'd collected. Two or three armed deputies normally accompanied them during these excursions. The Tennessee River wasn't far, but given the state of the neighborhood, the trip could still be dangerous.

One of the deputies who had helped bring Tray in told John he'd been there and seen the whole thing. "We were parked by the river's edge and they were filling buckets of water when the shots rang out. Susan was the first to get hit and she fell into the water. We tried to return fire, but we just couldn't match them."

He was talking about the pistols and deer rifles they were using against semi-autos.

"All I know is four people are dead by the river and one of them is Deputy Alex."

"Alex Winters?" John asked.

The man nodded.

Alex was from the very first training class. A nineteen-year-old kid who might have made it to the NHL if the EMP hadn't hit. Now he was dead and Cain and his thugs were likely to blame.

Susan Wheeler was another loss they couldn't afford. In spite of her high-strung personality, she'd run the water retrieval operation like a well-oiled machine. Now someone new would need to take her place and John wondered if they'd be nearly as efficient.

While the wounded were being patched up, John took eight well-armed deputies and went to retrieve the dead. Part of him hoped Cain's men were still there. As much as it was against his better judgment, he couldn't help wishing for an opportunity to seek out vengeance for what those animals had done.

By the time they got there, only three bodies were visible. Deputy Alex and the two members of Susan's team. All were dead. Susan herself, who the surviving deputy had said had fallen into the river, was nowhere to be seen. More than likely her body had been swept downstream and left to snag on some jagged outcropping of rock or an overhanging tree branch.

It was becoming crystal clear that a war had started. Abraham Lincoln had once said that God could not be for and against the same thing at the same time. The thought was at once sobering and heartening since it was difficult to believe He could be on the side of Cain and his gang of criminals. How all of this would turn out John didn't know, but one thing was becoming clear. When the smoke finally cleared, only one group would remain standing.

Chapter 32

That evening, John had descended into the pod with Diane, Gregory and Emma to say goodnight. For them, sleeping down here was now more important than ever following Cain's attack on Susan and the members of the water retrieval team.

There would need to be some kind of funeral in the morning. Right now the community was on high alert until further notice. Going down to the Tennessee River for water was now off limits. The committee would elect a new resident to take on Susan's responsibilities and additional hands to replace the folks who had been killed. From now on they would stick to draining the water heaters from houses on nearby streets. Those were supposed to be their last-ditch reserves in case of emergency. Well, the emergency had finally arrived.

John kissed Emma's forehead as she lay in her bunk. He then went to Gregory and did the same. The frailty of a human life had been driven home several times today. From now on, he would kiss his wife and children whenever he got the chance, knowing it might be his last.

Finally he came to Diane. She wasn't tired, he could tell—not physically tired, although emotionally, all of them were drained.

John took her in his arms and hugged her.

"Promise me you'll get us out of here before things get too out of hand."

He pulled away and stared at her, not entirely able to maintain eye contact. "You know I can't make that promise."

"A little voice inside me keeps saying we should have left straight away."

"But how could we have known it would come to this?" he cut her off. "I'm sure there are plenty of other groups within a ten-mile radius scraping by without a guy like Cain threatening to harm them."

"We got a bum deal, is what you're saying?"

"I'm saying we made a choice based on the information we had at the time. If we hadn't stayed and helped organize these people, how long would any of them lasted? At least now they have a fighting chance. You saw what Cain did to the others around us who didn't band together."

"I know," she whispered. "That's what I'm afraid of."

"Maybe you're right," John said, hating what it would do for Willow Creek's morale if he and his family were to up and leave. It would look like they had decided to cut and run and maybe that was exactly how Diane was feeling, but their marriage had always been a partnership, not a dictatorship.

The community would be shocked and disappointed, no doubt about it. But his responsibility to them had always been a distant second to the responsibility he felt for his family.

"Okay, tomorrow I'll call a committee meeting and make the announcement that we're leaving. I'm sure Peter and Frank will be able to fill my shoes quite nicely. I suppose getting the ball rolling was more than I could have asked for."

The muffled sound of gunfire from topside made all of their heads snap to attention. Then came the distinct boom from the Barrett M107 being fired, followed seconds later by the fog horn. One short blast at first. Then two and finally three.

The first two meant the barricades were under attack. The last meant the perimeter had been breached.

Chapter 33

John scrambled up the ladder and slammed the hatch shut just as Diane yelled after him.

With his pistol already on him, John grabbed his chest rig and Colt AR-15. A second later he was up the basement stairs and on the main floor, heading for one of the front windows so he could assess the situation.

The echo from sporadic gunfire rattled the window panes. It was dark outside, but the western barricade by Pine Grove was still visible. Three deputies stood in a squared stance, firing their rifles at an old tractor that was charging toward them. It had a shovel on the front which it had raised to deflect their bullets. They continued firing until the last minute when the tractor crashed through the barricade.

Sheet metal flew in the air and the two cars that covered the street were flung apart from the impact. There was a blur of destruction as the barricade was left with a gaping hole.

Another shot from Frank's Barrett rang out, cutting through the tractor's windshield and killing the driver. It veered off and rolled another few feet until it hit the curb and stopped. The tractor was out of action, but the damage had already been done. A handful of Cain's men swarmed in, killing the deputies wounded when the barricade was breached.

Outside was sheer pandemonium. People from both sides ran in every direction. Residents fired down on the attackers from the second-story windows of their homes. Deputies positioned on key rooftops were also engaging Cain's men. A handful of deputies in the foxhole were pinned down by enemy fire.

John was getting ready to fire from his dining-room window when figures across the street darted from between the houses. Cain's men had breached the back fences and were coming in from all directions. Some must have broken into the houses from the rear because the supporting fire from the second-story windows stopped.

A blur tore past John's own window. The same was happening on his side. Glass shattered in the living room. He and Gregory had spent the entire first day after the EMP boarding up all the back windows and creating a funnel in his home that would lead to a kill zone. The purpose had been to avoid precisely what was happening all over Willow Creek now—Cain's men storming in from all sides and smashing through back windows to deny the residents the use of prepared firing positions. Whoever had come to attack his house had clearly seen the boarded windows and decided to attack from the front.

John scrambled back toward the kitchen and the AR500 ballistic steel plate that would block their path. The plate had been fashioned with firing holes to enable John to fill the hallway with either slugs or double-ought buck from his Kel-Tec KSG shotgun as they approached. The shotgun was leaning up against the side wall. John shouldered his AR and grabbed the shotgun and then swung the metal plate closed. It clanged shut, vibrating in his hands just as screams of pain echoed from the living room. The attackers climbing through the windows had

163

found the razor wire gift he'd left for them. The stuff could cut to the bone and any man wounded badly enough wouldn't be able to use or operate a weapon afterward without getting the proper medical attention.

John racked the Kel-Tec and set the selector switch to double-ought buck. An old claymore bag converted to hold shotgun shells was on the kitchen table, filled with buckshot and one-ounce slugs. He would start by peppering the hallway as they came on and then switch to the slugs once they got closer.

Receiving one of those in the chest at close range was like being struck by a tiny cannonball. He'd seen a one-ounce slug hit a brown bear once on a hunting trip and watched it go right through the animal's ribcage and out the other end. If it could do that to a thousand-pound brown bear, what would it do to a two-hundred-pound man?

John pulled on the helmet lying on his kitchen table and brought the PVS-14 nightvision monocle down over his eye, drowning the room in green light.

The first thug came tearing out of the living room, carrying a pump-action shotgun. But the business end of John's boom stick was already pointing down the hallway.

John squeezed the trigger. The kitchen and hall exploded with light and a deafening blast as the buckshot ripped into the attacker's chest and flung him back. John racked it just in time for the next attacker. Another loud boom from his Kel-Tec and this time it struck the man in the gut, dropping him to the floor as he screamed in agony. John quickly switched to the one-ounce slugs and racked the shotgun again.

A third man in the living room peered out and John fired at his head, missing by inches, but punching a three-inch hole in the drywall. A second later an object came rolling down the hallway and clanged against the metal shield. The distinct sound the object made travelling down the hall was enough to tell John it was a grenade.

He dove for cover inside the laundry room adjacent to the kitchen. Combat training had taught him to keep his body as low as possible since a frag grenade tended to explode up and out. The concussion hit a second later, blowing the shield off its hinges and tossing it against the back kitchen wall.

Blood rolled out from John's ears. He hoped his eardrums hadn't been damaged in the explosion. His goggles were off and by his side. Patting himself all over, he realized that he hadn't been hit by any of the shrapnel.

A moment later, he was back on his feet, the AR front and center now. Cain's men had stormed into his neighborhood, into his house and thought they could harm his family. John was about to let them know they'd made a terrible mistake.

The one who'd just thrown the grenade was in the hallway coming toward him, a pistol in his hand. John fired the S&W, squeezing off four shots before the man fell dead.

The one he'd hit in the gut with the shotgun moments before was pulling himself along the floor, heading for the front entrance. John used the pistol to finish him off. Soon it was clear that all of Cain's men who'd stormed his house were dead, but the violence outside was still raging.

John exited via the front door, a move his tactical training suggested wasn't a great idea, but right now, climbing through the windows he'd laced with razor wire would have made even less sense.

The sight that greeted him outside was hellish. Three houses across the street were on fire, along with two on his side. One of those belonged to Al, and John hoped to God he and Missy weren't still inside.

The deputies in the foxhole were still being pinned down and John made it his mission to get them back into the fight. He moved rapidly away from the burning house to keep his position hidden and took cover at the base of a nearby tree. From there he spotted the muzzle flash from the guns keeping his men trapped. The shots were coming from the western barricade. John zeroed in with his Trijicon scope on three men with automatic rifles. Frank's Barrett M107 hadn't sounded off since the tractor had burst through their defenses and John hoped his friend had managed to reposition himself.

The AR kicked slightly as John placed rounds against his targets, killing one man outright and wounding another. The third scrambled for cover, but he couldn't outrun a bullet and down he went. Then John realized a fourth man had been with them and in the firelight from the burning houses, he saw that it was Cain. Four more shots rang out from John's AR, but each of them narrowly missed as Cain sprinted around obstacles, heading for the line of houses.

John rose and chased after him. Other battles were going on around him. The deputies at last were able to emerge from the foxhole and began fighting back.

The heat from Al's burning house was intense and the feeling running past it was like running your hand over a BBQ pit. Up ahead, Cain disappeared into the Hectors' house. By the time John arrived a moment later, threads of orange flame and black smoke had already begun to spill out of the broken front windows. Cain must have lit the drapes on fire soon after entering.

He was trying to deter anyone from coming after him. A technique that might have worked on a regular man, but not John.

AR at the ready, John circled around back and entered the house through a yellow door. It led in

166

through the Hectors' garage. The important point was to avoid being where Cain was expecting him. He also wanted to ensure the drug-dealing thug hadn't tried to escape through the backyard.

Inside, the ceiling was beginning to fill with black smoke. John moved purposefully from room to room, AR at the ready. It wasn't the ideal weapon for close quarters, but he could have his S&W out of his drop-leg holster and in his hands in a split second if he needed to.

A figure zipped by him ten yards away and fled up the stairs to the second floor. John didn't have enough time to take a clean shot and didn't want to give his presence away just yet. He wanted to see the surprise on Cain's face when he sent the man back to hell.

John grabbed a dishtowel from a rack in the kitchen and held it over his nose. He then proceeded toward the stairs and began mounting them. He would need to get this done quick since the fire downstairs was beginning to grow.

After reaching the top riser, John scanned the landing without seeing any sign of his target. Checking each bedroom was his next priority. He was about to enter the first when he heard a noise to his right. Cain was there about to fire his AK-47. John dropped to one knee, aimed in that direction and fired. The shots narrowly missed, blasting holes in the wall by Cain's head. Splinters of wood and gyprock blinded Cain and he fell back into one of the front bedrooms. As he did, the AK fell from his hands and landed in the hallway.

Weapon or not, this was a dangerous place to be since the fire raging below them was directly underneath the room Cain had retreated to. John pressed on nevertheless. He needed to finish this, even if it meant further risking his own life.

Black smoke inched down at him from the ceiling. John did his best to keep low.

When John reached the doorway, he saw Cain fiddling madly with a stuck window. Perhaps sensing him there, Cain turned and immediately charged toward John.

John squeezed the trigger right as the floor at Cain's feet gave way, swallowing him whole. Flames licked up through the opening as though John's prediction had been right and hell itself had taken him back.

John turned and began to make his way downstairs to be sure the job was done. When he reached the first floor the flames in the front of the house where Cain had fallen through were raging out of control. No one could have survived that and John decided to retreat and help with the other beleaguered defenders before he was overcome by fumes. Surely with their leader gone, the criminals' will to fight would die as well.

Chapter 34

The scene that greeted John was one of complete carnage. The bodies of friend and foe lay side by side, an image that reminded him of accounts from the Civil War. Soldiers had often described the dead being so thick they could walk from one end of a battlefield to the other without touching the ground.

There was enough space between each of the houses that the fires wouldn't jump, but already three homes across the street were reduced to smoldering ash. So was Al's house.

Here and there, sporadic gunfire broke the eerie silence, but the peak of the battle had passed. Now that Cain was gone, John rushed back to his own house so that it too wasn't torched. The pod was designed to be fireproof, that wasn't the problem. It was the oxygen getting cut off in the event of a fire that worried him most.

When he was nearly there, dark figures ran toward the park on their way out of Willow Creek. They were carrying jugs of water and large sacks presumably stuffed with canned goods. He lowered himself onto one knee, peered through his Trijicon ACOG scope and shot three of them dead. The last managed to dart behind cover before he could finish the job.

The street was in complete shambles. With Cain dead and his thugs on the run, it appeared the people of Willow Creek had won, but at what cost? No one would know until dawn when they would begin to tally their losses.

•••

John slept slumped in a chair in his kitchen, the Kel-Tec KSG laid across his lap. He'd dragged the dented steel plate back into place and waited for the light to come. There'd been an eerie silence outside and John couldn't help wonder which of his friends and neighbors had survived.

Finally, faint light began to trickle in through the now shattered front windows. John peered outside for any signs of Cain's men. The prospect was doubtful. He would have heard them looting and pillaging throughout the night but all he'd heard was deathly silence.

The sight outside was sobering. Men and women with red bandanas mixed with Cain's thugs were dead and scattered for as far as John could see. A few stunned figures had emerged from their homes, most of them bloody. They staggered among the dead, weeping. It really did look like a battlefield and when things were finally put right, John hoped there would be some sort of memorial here to the people who'd given up their lives for the right to live without fear of oppression.

John went down to the pod and got Diane and the kids. They were visibly frightened and had stayed up throughout the night. Even buried underground, they'd still heard the battle going on topside. They were sure no one was left and John didn't have the heart to tell them that they might be right.

"Oh, your ears," Diane said when she saw the blood. "We heard the explosion and thought the house had been hit by an RPG."

"You're not too far from the truth," he told her. "But my hearing's already coming back."

"Did we win at least, Dad?" Gregory asked.

John ruffled his son's hair. "It looks that way, son, but we paid a heavy price."

The concern on Diane's face intensified. Her worst fears had become a reality.

The idea of going upstairs and letting his kids see what lay outside was gut-wrenching. No child should see that. But there was no way around it. They would need to find the survivors and salvage what they could. Cain and his men seemed to have been defeated, but who knew what other groups were out there waiting to take his place.

No words could soften the blow, it was simply something they would have to experience.

He brought them upstairs and when he opened the front door they gasped. Tears streamed down Diane's face. Her hands went to her quivering lips. "Oh God, John. Oh God."

A handful of others were outside now, checking on the bodies, engaged in the gruesome task of sorting the dead from the wounded. There weren't many of the latter.

After that was done, John quickly organized the people he could find into search parties who went house to house, trying to find more survivors who'd hidden from the battle. In all, twenty people were left. Twenty residents of Willow Creek out of over a hundred.

The cost of victory was staggering. But it was only when they began counting the dead that two things became apparent.

The first was that Cain had lost nearly two hundred men.

The second was that Al and Missy were nowhere to be found.

Diane pointed to their house, which was now a heap of ashes. "That's probably where they are."

Emma sobbed, burying her face in her mother's arms. Not simply from the loss of their long-time neighbors. The enormity of the situation had finally hit home and the weight of it had been too much.

Bill Kelsaw, his head wrapped in a bandage, came up to John. "Hell on earth," he said.

John nodded. What else could he say?

"What about Frank and Peter?" John asked.

Bill's eyes dropped. "I found them over there." He pointed to the tree stand. "They put up one hell of a fight, that's all I'll say."

John closed his eyes and said a silent prayer.

"I won't be staying," Bill said. "Not anymore. There's nothing left. We beat them back, but we've got nothing left."

He was right and Diane knew it too. They could stay here and spend precious time digging a pit to bury all the dead, or they could leave Willow Creek behind and head for the safety of the cabin.

John didn't need to ask Diane what she thought, nor the kids. The answer was obvious.

Chapter 35

The family's bug-out bags were already in the Blazer. That was something John had made sure of the very first day in case they needed to get out of Knoxville in a hurry.

The next hour was spent transferring other essentials. The food stored in the pod, as well as the canned items Diane had prepared early on. First-aid supplies, weapons, ammo and water. Other items like the pressure canner, jerrycans with diesel and Coleman lanterns and batteries were also included. The list was a long one and it took some ingenuity to squeeze it all into Betsy. Course, after the EMP hit, the Ford F-150 had become little more than a giant paperweight. A pity really because it halved the amount they could bring with them.

As it was, they were each leaving behind dozens of items of emotional significance. Photo albums were nice, but they could never take the place of a rifle or filtered water.

Once Betsy was packed, John went out and spoke with the other survivors. He made sure they had the food and water they needed. Bill Kelsaw said he would be heading to Nashville to look for his sister, who he hadn't spoken to since the collapse. Others had a similar plan. There was no point in staying on Willow Creek, not anymore. John was just glad he'd listened to his gut and stayed. Every armed man and woman had counted last night and without any one of them, the battle might have turned out differently. The worst-case scenario would have been Cain's forces rolling in with little or no opposition. Then what would have become of those who remained? A terrifying thought indeed. Grim as it was, at least now they had a chance.

The sad truth was that most of the survivors didn't have a secret bug-out cabin in the hills they could escape to. But taking them all with him just wasn't an option. With rationing, he and his family could survive on what was in the cabin, along with the supplies from the house, for over a year. Water would be the tricky part, but a stream nearby would act as a plentiful source. A source they would need to filter and purify.

Taking another look at those assembled before him, John was struck by one other thing. Not a single member of the committee besides himself had survived. Al, Arnold, Curtis, Wendy and even Patty were all gone. Those who remained stood together and said a final prayer for the fallen and a few words for the future.

With some help from Bill and the others they removed the dead from the street. This was where the Blazer would be coming through on its way out of Sequoyah Hills and running over his old friends was an indignity they didn't deserve. It was bad enough they would be denied a proper burial.

After they'd finished that terrible job, John and Bill stood for a minute, John wiping the sweat off his brow, Bill fanning his t-shirt to cool himself.

"How long you figure it'll take you to reach that cabin of yours up near Oneida?" Bill asked.

John stared at him in shock, trying his best not to let his face betray how he was feeling. "What cabin, Bill?" He wasn't one for playing games. The idea that their secret bug-out location wasn't such a secret after all left him feeling numb.

"Oh, all right, John, my mistake then."

"Who told you I had a cabin?"

"Just a rumor, John. I think Curtis mentioned it to me. That you had a place up in the Appalachians stocked with food and water."

Now John was getting angry. That cabin was the difference between life and death for his family and wasn't something to be discussed among neighbors. More than that, John wanted to know how word of it had leaked out. Could Diane have said something to Patty or someone else in her group?

"Didn't mean to upset you, John," Bill said, pausing briefly before clapping him on the shoulder. "Your secret's safe with me. Forget I even brought it up."

John nodded, feeling the sudden blinding need to speak to his wife and find the source of the leak.

•••

John and his family left an hour later. The trip itself was going to be dangerous. Betsy was a great, reliable truck that was up for the challenge, but she wasn't armored. John had opted for speed and fuel economy rather than building himself a tank. Sure, a Brinks truck might have made the ultimate bug-out vehicle, but it didn't hold a candle to Betsy in the fuel-efficiency category.

In Diane's lap sat a Beretta 9mm and the Kel-Tec KSG shotgun loaded with double-ought buck. Since he was driving, John carried his S&W. The AR was nearby however, snuggled between the console and Diane's seat. If things got hairy, he could have it on target in seconds.

The truth was, John wasn't expecting many ambushes once they hit the interstate. Most everyone was either on foot or using bikes now. A truck barreling by would be a rare sight indeed.

Getting out of Knoxville—that would be the dangerous part.

The highways in town were still cluttered with stalled cars. As a result, the goal was to use the major boulevards and streets in order to hit the interstate on the outskirts of town. There John hoped it would prove less congested.

It had been a little over a week since the lights had gone out and already the city looked completely different. Many of the houses had boards over the windows, others were burned out.

The fires he knew weren't all from vandals and thugs. Millions of people all over had likely turned to candles. After the first few days, some of them would have become careless and that was when fires started. Without any firefighters, buildings that went up in flames would have suffered the same fate as the ones on Willow Creek and the surrounding neighborhoods.

The memory of seeing Al's house with the bodies of him and his wife still inside, burnt to a crisp, was still fresh in John's mind.

Sad how long it took to build something worthwhile and how quickly all that hard work could be turned to ash. It was true for Willow Creek as much as it was true for the country as a whole.

Cumberland Avenue led to an interstate on-ramp. They were far enough on the outskirts of Knoxville that John guessed the highway would be relatively clear. If their current location was any indication, then they would be fine. John had kept a hand on the pistol that was resting in the console's cupholder, releasing it every so often when he needed both hands to navigate around a car blocking his path. Up to this point, however, he hadn't seen a soul. Surely the noise of Betsy's diesel engine was attracting attention, but if faces had popped out of doorways after they sped by, John hadn't seen them.

The on-ramp appeared on his right and John went up it. Just as he suspected, the traffic leaving the city was light, giving him plenty of room to bob and weave between the few stalled cars that were there.

The lanes in the opposite direction were another story entirely. Those were packed to the gills and many of the vehicles had open doors where drivers and passengers had simply decided to continue on foot. So far he hadn't seen anyone in cars or along the highway's shoulder. But it was only a question of time. He'd seen plenty of dead in his combat tours and plenty more over the last twenty-four hours. Soldier or not, the sight was never one you relished, not unless you were missing the important parts God gave you.

The Mack family continued their trek to the cabin, driving for another thirty minutes before they finally saw another soul. Two people actually, a man and a woman, walking along the interstate pushing a shopping cart packed with supplies covered by a blue tarp. Predictably, one of the cart's front wheels was doing a merry jig, probably giving the man pushing the thing a terrible time.

As they approached, Diane lowered the window and held the pistol against the outside of the passenger door. The point was to send them a clear message—we're armed and ready to shoot, but not if you mind your own business. Gun-barrel diplomacy. Who knew that the way you held a gun could say so much?

The couple stood still and watched as the Blazer approached, as though they were observing a mirage or something divine. The woman used her hand to block out the sun, low in the early-morning sky, squinting at the truck and its lucky occupants.

Diane nodded to them and they waved back. They seemed like nice enough people. John hoped they would stay safe.

Soon enough they came upon another group. This one consisted of five people, a real mishmash, making it difficult to tell if they were from the same family or had banded together to travel. Safety in numbers was surely the new law of the land.

"They're all heading into the country," Diane exclaimed.

"The legendary golden horde," John murmured. "And right on time, too. Most of the preppers woulda left within a day or two. Normal folks expecting FEMA or the local government to swoop in and save the day would have waited much longer before running out of food and realizing they'd been wrong. When they slowly realized that no one was coming to save them, and with empty cupboards and bare shelves in the grocery store, what other options did they have?"

"They're going where the food is."

John shook his head. "They're going where they *think* the food is. But these stragglers are going to be disappointed. The folks in the country will be struggling to manage their crops. They also rely on automated systems and vehicles, all of which don't work anymore. They'll be better off than the urban elites, no doubt about that. But it certainly won't be the bountiful harvest these refugees are expecting."

It wasn't long before they came to an even larger group walking along the interstate's shoulder. This time, hearing them approach, a few began moving toward them, shaking their clasped hands together. It was a sight more common in the streets of India as beggars rushed to car windows in search of a handout.

"Tell them to back off," John told her.

Diane raised the pistol, but didn't fire. With her free hand she was motioning for the few rushing to cut them off to back away. John stepped on the pedal and accelerated past them.

"That could have turned ugly," Diane said. She hadn't ever killed another human being. He'd always appreciated her compassion, but in the current climate he needed to know she could drop someone if the situation called for it. He told her as much.

She didn't like the comment since it questioned her commitment.

"I just need to know if push comes to shove, you'd be willing to kill a man."

"Or a woman," she added.

The point was true. He'd always assumed that if there was an aggressor it would be a man, a target he wouldn't have as much difficulty dispatching. Proof of his resolve lay dead in the street of their old neighborhood and in combat zones around the world. He was trained for such things, she wasn't. Sure, he'd taught her all the important skill sets, but making it over that final hump was another matter entirely. Right now that was the question mark.

"I'd do it," Gregory said from the back seat.

"I know you would, son," John answered.

Emma didn't say a word. She wasn't interested in proving herself nearly as much as Gregory was. He was becoming more like his dad every day. The cleft in his chin, the strong jaw and cheekbones. His son was still at the age where he idolized his father.

179

Then in the distance, John caught sight of something which froze the blood in his veins. A huge mass of refugees moving northwest. This was likely the vanguard of the golden horde. A city on the move, an exodus toward the perceived safety of the lush countryside. But these guys weren't only on the shoulder. They were spread all over and John wasn't entirely sure they'd be quick to move out of his way. If a crowd like this got angry, things could turn deadly in a heartbeat.

A few of them turned and pointed as the truck approached. Maybe they thought it was FEMA coming to save them. If so, they were in for a nasty disappointment. John began to accelerate and honk the horn. A few began to move away, afraid of being run over.

But the bulk of them kept marching on.

"You're gonna need to give them some encouragement, honey," John said. "If anyone gets aggressive, shoot them."

She swallowed hard, raised the pistol and fired three shots into the air. That got their attention and the crowd began to disperse in a giant wave, some moving to the shoulder, others jumping the median and scattering onto the other side of the highway. A handful of John Wayne types were feeling stubborn. John lowered the window, aimed his pistol about six feet over their heads and laid off three more shots. Betsy charged forward, barely slowing down. At the very last minute they jumped out of the way. If those people thought their lives held such little value, John had no compunction about separating them from it.

They rocketed past the crowd, which had parted for them like the Red Sea for Moses.

The size of this horde moving northwest didn't worry John too much. This was precisely why he'd selected a bug-out location that was away from the major highways and thoroughfares. That sort of thing was in nearly every prepper 101 guide. Everyone knew when the cities emptied, people fleeing the chaos and the danger would use the country's main arteries as their primary routes of escape.

They would move across the land like a swarm of locusts, devouring everything before them. That was the prediction some had made and here it was coming true. He hadn't exactly witnessed a swath of destruction in their wake, but a group like that needed to eat something and when they did they were liable to empty entire farms in one sitting. It was an army and John was just glad it would surge right past the side roads which led to the cabin.

Chapter 36

Not long after that they turned off Interstate 75 North and followed State Route 63 West. Rocks and gravel crunched under the Blazer's tires as they travelled along country roads. The scenery in the area was breathtaking. Lush forests and rolling hills. The air warm and clean.

In the past couple of years, the family had been to the cabin about half a dozen times, mostly during bug-out drills when John had timed them to see how long it would take to make the trip from A to Z. During each trip they'd brought up sacks of grains, powdered milk, wholewheat flour, yeast, baking soda and other food they could store. They'd also set up a water filtration system using two fifty-gallon drums and an impressive underground storage unit. The process was simple enough. One drum was placed on top of the other. Holes were poked in the bottom of the top drum and filled with alternating layers of sand and charcoal. These would help to strain the larger impurities. What collected in the bottom drum would then be boiled to kill any remaining harmful bacteria.

Another few minutes up the gravel path brought them to the private road which led to the cabin. It was only one of three cabins on this side of the mountain, which meant very little traffic came up that dirt road. When he had time, John and Gregory would come down and lay some obstacles over the path. A log would work. Either way it needed to be something that could block a vehicle from driving right up to the cabin's front door. In addition, John would also look at camouflaging the turnoff to his cabin. That way it might hide them from would-be attackers or raiders looking for an easy target to plunder.

Up to now, most of John's energy had been spent supplying the cabin with food and an ability to filter water. More weekends up here would have meant more time to build defenses and booby-traps. In the end it meant he and Gregory and the girls would need to hustle.

Betsy hummed as she clawed her way up the steep dirt path. A second later the cabin came into full view. A smile spread over John's face. She was a sight for sore eyes. The eye in the great storm that was tearing the country to shreds. And that was when his smile began to fade.

Diane was already pointing at the cabin. "John, am I imagining things or is that smoke coming from the chimney?"

He slammed the brakes and stared, trying to make sense of what he was seeing.

Before him was a simple, two-story wood beam log cabin. John had liked that idea since the sixteen-inch walls would stop small-caliber rounds. Two windows on the main floor. One on the top floor for each of the three bedrooms. There was room enough for each member of his family, but the smoke coming out of his chimney meant someone else had stumbled onto the cabin and claimed it for themselves.

There wasn't any sign of a car or even bikes out front, but those things could just as easily be parked in the open space behind the cabin. There also weren't any police or local sheriffs John could call. It was every man for himself and every prepper's nightmare. John backed the Blazer up until it was just beyond view.

"What are we gonna do, Dad?" Gregory and Emma asked at almost the exact same time.

Diane was looking at him with a "what now" sort of look. They all wanted to know and their panic and fear was making it hard for him to think straight.

"You three stay here," John said as he got out and went to the back of the truck. Once there he opened the hatch and removed his tactical vest and two-point sling. In the front mag pouches were four thirty-round magazines for his AR. The S&W was already in his drop-leg holster.

Gregory turned around. "You gonna go blow them away, Dad?"

John shook his head. "I hope I don't have to. But one way or another, whoever's in our cabin is about to get an eviction notice."

He closed the hatch quietly and went back to the driver's side where Diane handed him the AR which he clipped to the sling.

"Fall back if you're outnumbered," she told him.

"I will, honey. You just be ready with that shotgun in case I do. Love you."

Chapter 37

A million scenarios were running through John's head as he approached the cabin. The front windows were dark, making it impossible to see how many intruders were inside. He set himself up along the tree line next to a patch of overgrowth and dug around for some rocks. He would start by throwing them at the cabin door and wait to see who came out.

The first two rocks skittered over the front porch. The next two struck dead on, creating a loud bang. A face appeared briefly in the window and John removed the safety on his AR and took aim. Then the face disappeared and the door opened. A single figure stood silhouetted in the doorway. It was a man and he was holding a small-caliber pistol.

"I've got you dead to rights," John said. "Now set the gun down and kick it away before I blow your head off."

The man hesitated.

"I know what you're thinking," John continued. "You're wondering whether you can slam that door shut in time. I promise that you can't. Now do as I say before I drop you right now. Do it!"

The man complied.

"Kick the gun away."

He did.

"Is there anyone else in there with you? And don't even think of lying to me."

"Yes," the man said. He sounded scared. Fear was exactly what John wanted him to feel. Fear was what gummed up all the works in men's brains, prevented them from thinking straight. Humans tended to fall back on their instinctual habit of following orders when that happened. It was why police stormed a suspect's house shouting for them to drop their weapons.

"How many others?"

"Three."

"Men or women?"

"My wife and two kids."

John wanted to curse, but bit his lip. Why couldn't it have been a group of bandits instead of a family?

"This is private property and you have no business being here."

The man in the doorway paused and then said, "John? Is that you?"

Now it was John's turn to be stunned and surprised.

The man came into the light and John's jaw nearly dropped.

Standing before him was Tim Appleby.

•••

Minutes later the two families were in the kitchen and the awkwardness was thick enough to cut with a Bowie knife. The only ones who were happy with the present situation were Emma and Brandon. She'd practically jumped into his arms, tears running down her face.

John wasn't the least bit happy with any of it, especially the long hugs Emma and Brandon kept sharing. The Applebys didn't seem to mind those. In fact,

186

they thought it was cute. Maybe if it was their daughter instead of his, they might not have been so keen.

The rest of them stood around, Diane trying to catch John's eye, to tell him as usual to be nice.

"Would you like some coffee?" Kay Appleby asked.

She was only trying to be polite, but being treated like a guest in his own home by people who'd broken in and been eating his food for days was boiling John's blood something awful. Diane put a hand on him and he shook it off.

"Let me start by saying I'm happy none of you were hurt," John began. "The rest of us on Willow Creek thought you'd been kidnapped by Cain and his men."

"Cain?" Tim asked, looking puzzled.

"A real bad man," Diane said. "John... killed him."

"His thugs were probably the ones who broke into your home. We assumed the worst the next day when you were gone. Your car was missing too. Figured you'd been killed or carted off for God knows what."

"The car's here," Tim said sheepishly. "Parked it around back so no one would see it."

John drew in a deep breath. "What I really wanna know is how you found out about the cabin in the first place. And how you knew how to get here."

Tim hesitated and then seeing the deadly seriousness on John's face acquiesced. "Brandon told us."

John and Diane both looked to Emma at the same time.

If looks could kill.

"I didn't mean to," Emma started, unable to maintain eye contact.

"Yes, you did," Diane cut her off. "But don't bother with excuses, we'll discuss it later."

"Here's the thing, Tim. If you'd been anyone else I probably would have shot you dead. You broke into my

187

house. Been living here for a better part of a week. We could have also run away, but instead we chose to stay and help defend Willow Creek from a pack of drug-dealing murderers."

"I'm sorry, John. I didn't know what else to do."

"You should have stayed. That's what I'm telling you. You fled when you didn't need to. When the community needed you the most."

Tim's eyes fell. "So why are you here now? I mean, what changed your mind?"

John didn't know if he'd be able to say it.

"We were attacked last night," Diane told them. "By Cain and a couple hundred of his men. Most of them were killed, but so too was nearly everyone on our street."

Kay burst into tears. "Oh, no. How horrible."

"At least they went out fighting," John said. "Those who lived one street over didn't pull together quickly enough and became refugees. Most of them were killed on their way to the interstate. Cut down like lambs to the slaughter."

"I hate to admit it, but we were afraid, John, and that's why we fled."

"Well, that's all ancient history," John said. "Right now we got a situation on our hands. The cabin's only got a supply of food for four people. I'm assuming you didn't bring any of your own."

Tim shook his head.

"So then you've already started into ours."

"Just a little bit," Kay said, trying to minimize it.

What she didn't know was there were two stockpiles John had created. The first was the main one hidden away in a cold room accessed through the crawlspace under the cabin. The food Kay was talking about was the decoy. It still counted toward the year's supply, but was intended

188

to be what any thieves would grab instead of looking for the motherlode. That way they could survive a break-in if they were away and still keep the bulk of their preps.

"So you want us to leave," Tim said, pulling his wife and daughter Natalie in tight. Brandon stayed by Emma's side.

John didn't say a word right then, but that was exactly what he was thinking.

Chapter 38

John and Diane went off to discuss it. Emma tried following them, intent on putting her two cents in, but there wasn't much need for that. It was clear enough Brandon was the reason she'd wanted to stay on Willow Creek so badly in the beginning and why she would now try and convince them to let the Applebys remain.

"I think I know what you're going to say," Diane said first, taking John by the hand.

He smiled. "You know me so well, don't you?"

"After sixteen years of marriage, a woman learns a thing or two about her husband."

"I'm all ears."

She released his hand and became serious. "You want them to go, maybe more than you're letting on. You want them to offer to leave on their own, rather than forcing us to turf them out."

"So far so good."

"You've always been a firm man, but I've never known you to be unfair. I think it was incredibly difficult when you were forced to turn those neighbors at the barricades away and then listen to them being slaughtered."

John nodded, staring off. "I've seen similar scenes play out in Third World countries as one tribal group turned on another even after the United States was called

190

in to play peacekeeper. Our rules of engagement prevented us from getting directly involved in local disputes. That feeling of having your hands tied behind your back while bad men do terrible things is something I've never forgotten. I'd hoped it would be different at home if ever there was a collapse, but I see now it was exactly the same. And there I was again, hands tied while innocent people were marched off to die."

"I can't imagine," she said. "It must have been awful."

"I said I'd never let it happen again, but when the time came and I had to choose between the safety of others and the safety of my family, I made the same choice."

"You can't take responsibility for that, John. The council outvoted you. If you'd have ignored the vote, their authority would effectively have been destroyed. Besides, those refugees made the choice not to prepare for the worst. That wasn't your fault."

He squeezed her hand. "I know. I've been telling myself that ever since. Every man makes his own bed. I don't weep for the men and women who didn't plan ahead. But I can still see that man trying to pass his child over the barricade. Those children never made that choice."

"The sins of the father," Diane said.

John nodded. "We also have another issue. Before we left, Bill Kelsaw let it slip that he knew about the cabin."

Diane's eyes grew wide. "If Bill knows then everyone knows."

"That's what I was thinking. He said he'd heard about it from Curtis, but that he wasn't sure where he'd gotten it from."

"Obviously Emma must have mentioned something to Brandon," Diane said. "She was probably trying to let

191

him know that if our family disappeared in the night, that was where we were going."

"That old British saying from World War II comes to mind," John told her. "Loose lips…"

"Sink ships. Sometimes the best-laid preps can be undone by a casual slip. You don't think the remaining folks from Willow Creek will begin showing up, do you?"

"I'm not sure," John said. "I tried my best to downplay it, make Bill think there was no cabin, but I wouldn't put money on whether he bought the attempt. I suppose we'll find out in a week or so."

Diane looked at him quizzically.

"I figure without a car that's how long it would take to make it to the cabin on foot."

"Unless they bike."

"With all the gear they'd need to bring with them? Maybe you're right. Then I guess we'll find out in three or four days."

"Between now and then, what do you wanna do?" Diane asked.

John shook his head. "I'm revoking Emma's right to weigh in. She's broken my trust and if groups of city folk start showing up then she may have denied us the cabin as well."

Chapter 39

"I want to stress this arrangement is only temporary," John told both families in the cramped confines of the kitchen. "I've discussed it with Diane and neither of us were happy to find our bug-out location occupied. We've also had a conversation with Emma who understands now the gravity of what she's done. There's still a lot to do around the cabin to prepare defenses and sustenance. Each and every one of you will need to pull your own weight; I expect no less from the Applebys than I do from my family. Rationed food supplies are only half the challenge with so many living under one roof. The cabin was designed for the four of us. Now we have double that number. That means three bedrooms for eight people.

"Diane and I will take the master bedroom. Tim and Kay can have Emma's room. Brandon and Gregory will share the last room. Emma and Natalie will sleep on the pull-out couch in the living room."

Emma sighed heavily, but John didn't have an ounce of pity for her. She was the reason for the cramped space they were facing. She was lucky John didn't make her sleep in the truck. She would also be given extra chores. Within a week or two she would feel the full impact of her indiscretion.

Diane had warned him not to go too hard on her. He'd been tempted to bring out the strap his father had used on him. Pre-collapse that sort of thing would have been looked down upon, but John suspected as society slowly clawed its way out of danger, corporal punishment would become the norm once again. In effect, they were witnessing a return to the homesteading days of the nineteenth century. And along with the homesteading came the Wild West mentality that often led to innocent people getting killed. Preventing that was first on John's list. The cabin needed to withstand a direct assault and have contingency plans in the worst-case scenario.

From here John outlined his ideas for defending the cabin. A hundred-meter gravel path led from the cabin to the country road. There was a slight incline leading to the house. The forest had also been cleared for thirty yards around the cabin in all directions. That meant they had a decent field of fire from every angle.

The first layer of defense would be concealment. Marauders couldn't attack a place they didn't know existed. John had made the turnoff to the cabin purposely narrow for this very reason. With John's direction, the four kids gathered dead leaves and fallen branches and used that to litter the turnoff. The contrast between the color of the gravel path and the surrounding vegetation would be a dead giveaway. It was important that a group moving past, particularly in vehicles, wouldn't notice the opening as easily.

Afterward they used spades to dig out a series of small holes. With hand saws they cut down a few one- and two-year-old trees and fit them into the holes, filling in the empty space with gravel. The idea was to maintain the illusion that the forest continued on unbroken.

While the kids worked on concealment, John and Tim tackled the next layer of defense, preventing vehicles from driving up to the cabin. That part was simple enough. They used John's gas-powered chainsaw to fell a tree. They selected a spot fifty yards up the road where the ground sloped. That way the tree would fall across the road as they intended.

A nearly invisible access path through the forest, wide enough for a single vehicle at a time, would lead around the tree.

The idea, however, wasn't to prevent an assault. History and common sense had already shown that a determined enemy would come regardless of the obstacles in his way. The secret, which had worked quite well back at his home on Willow Creek, was to control where the enemy approached from. If an oncoming force was funneled into a narrow kill zone, they wouldn't stand a chance against high-powered rifles. Unlike in the movies, high-caliber bullets tended to pass through multiple unarmored bodies, a truth the machine-gunners in the trenches of World War I had learned to devastating effect.

Attackers on foot would try to approach the cabin from the cover of the tree line and this was an advantage John and Tim needed to deny them. Without miles of razor wire, the only other solution was to lay multiple man traps along the edge of the path. These would consist of nail boards and sharpened stakes concealed by brush. Included in the booby traps were shotgun-shell tripwires. The spray of buck shot would certainly mangle a man's legs, but more importantly, it would send a message that veering off the path was very bad for your health. Finally, the shotgun tripwires would help alert those in the cabin that someone was coming.

John had bought a dozen of them online before the collapse that he stored at the cabin. They were a simple, yet ingenious little device. A mounting plate with a spring-loaded firing pin. Once the wire was tripped, it pulled on a trigger which fired the shell.

After that was done, John and Tim set up prepared firing positions by hand-drilling gun ports in the cabin's walls. Afterward, they would begin filling sandbags and stacking them around the opening. An average-sized, densely packed sandbag when stacked next to the thick beams of the cabin walls could stop anything short of a .50 cal.

Meanwhile, Diane and Kay busied themselves with planting the garden out back and tending to the greenhouse. They'd already decided to use the greenhouse for tomatoes, cucumbers, squash, zucchini, peppers, peas, and green beans. This would give them a nice range of vitamins and minerals as well as a number of good hearty dishes. Some preppers had a tendency to stick to practical foods which could be easily stored without considering something as basic as taste. Eating the same tasteless slop every day might look good on paper, but living it was another matter entirely. The other often overlooked consideration was a balanced meal with the right vitamins. A diet of homemade bread and meat tended to overlook the human body's need for vitamin C. The vegetables in the greenhouse would help to solve many of those problems.

In the garden outside, Diane and Kay would plant perennials in much the same fashion they'd done on Willow Creek. John's mother always said: If something worked well, why mess with it?

The seeds themselves had been stored in labeled pouches inside glass jars and would last three years. Of course, additional seeds could always be cultivated from the existing crop which meant, as long as they weren't driven off their land, they could maintain a full garden indefinitely.

196

Everyone understood the need to hurry. The streams of refugees John and his family had seen along the interstate only served to drive the point home further. In spite their best efforts, someone would eventually find their bug-out location. It was important that when that time came, John and the others were ready for them.

Chapter 40

After two solid fifteen-hour days spent erecting the cabin's defenses, John's attention turned to firearms training. The Applebys hadn't been around when John had taken the residents of Willow Creek through a safety and handling course. It was also important that each member of their tiny community became proficient at quick-loading and firing an assortment of weapons. There might be a situation where an AR wasn't within arm's reach and so a deer rifle needed to do.

Brandon took to it right away and quickly became the fastest of the children at stripping and reassembling an AR. Not to be outdone, Emma was the fastest at reloading pistol magazines while Gregory was the most proficient with the long-gun reloads. Natalie was a little slower on each, but eager to learn.

Using paracord, nylon sleeving and HK clips, John fashioned two-point slings for each of the ARs. There were only two, along with a thousand rounds of 5.56 green-tip ammo. He would have felt comfortable with more, of course, but for now it would have to do. The shotguns were the toughest for the children, although they found the Kel-Teck KSG easier to use. The double cylinder which allowed a shooter to cycle between two different types of ammo was also a nice feature and one that had served John well when defending his home against Cain's men.

Next John dug into the kit he kept at the cabin and came out with orange signal whistles for everyone. There were giggles and laughter at first as many of them suddenly felt like lifeguards. But these were special naval whistles often attached to lifejackets. They issued a shrill hundred-and-two-decibel dual tone that could travel great distances.

Next John explained how they should be used. If anyone spotted a single individual or small group approaching the cabin via the path, they were to give one short blast. A large group two blasts. And for anyone seen anywhere near or past the tree line they were to issue three short blasts. Calling others for help for any other reason was one very long blast. They drilled on this for close to an hour before John felt they all understood.

With only a single fog horn on Willow Creek, their early warning system had been vulnerable to an enemy with a scoped weapon, taking out the one person who could alert the others. Now, each of them had the ability to send a warning to the others or call for help if required.

Each of the adults would also carry at least a pistol on them at all times. Again, this seemed like a no-brainer, but the additional weight was cumbersome to Kay and Diane as they sweated over tilling soil, planting seeds and creating a mesh enclosure so small animals wouldn't get at the crops.

The final element of the cabin's security was organizing watches. With so few of them, it became nearly impossible to tackle the massive volume of work that needed to get done if twenty percent or more of their work force was keeping an eye on things. John and the others reasoned that since they were all outside engaged with various projects and that they also each had the orange sea whistles, they could get away without patrols during the day. At night however, each of them would take turns staying awake in three-hour blocks. Armed with an AR, pistol and the PVS-14 nightvision monocle, the designated person on watch would remain in the cabin and do their best to stay alert. If anyone were to approach, they would use the whistle. The sound would be deafening indoors, but it was guaranteed to get the rest of them on their feet.

Diane's experience in the last days of Willow Creek with Patty Long's improvised medical clinic had honed her ability to clean and dress wounds, even remove bullets. Over the last year, John had also stockpiled enough peroxide, clean bandages, basic medical instruments (scalpels and dressing pliers) as well as QuikClot to open their own hospital ward.

With food, security and medical largely taken care of, the next item to be addressed was water. Last fall, John had installed a thousand-gallon water storage tank. It had a hose and hand pump designed to pull the water in the event of a grid-down situation. There was also a rainwater collection system that would add water back to the tanks or alternatively store it in external fifty-gallon drums. A few drops of bleach per gallon could be used on the rainwater if needed, but the water in the thousand-gallon storage tank was clean to drink. It would also double as their bathing and dish water. With so many of them now living under one roof, the discussion about water had been more about usage. As long as it rained the tank would be replenished. In a worst-case scenario, the many streams in northern Tennessee would do the trick, one of which ran a hundred yards behind the cabin.

•••

John had just finished checking the eavestroughs and cleaning out the fifty-gallon drum when he noticed Emma by herself, filling a sandbag. Sandbag was a misnomer since the bags weren't really filled with sand, they were filled with hard-packed dirt. The reason was a simple one; there wasn't a sandpit nearby. But these would do for now. Nevertheless, John was proud of how hard Emma was working.

He went over and offered to give her a hand.

"Sure," she said, not looking up.

"How you getting along with our guests?" he asked, grinning to himself.

"Fine."

"Not better than fine?"

She fought a smile. "Okay, really fine." She looked like she was about to say something, perhaps about how much she hated having to give up her room, and then thought better of it. "What about you?" Emma asked, shielding her eyes from the sun as she looked up at him.

John glanced over at Tim and Brandon sawing a fallen tree to make firewood and kindling. "I won't lie. Way better than I thought I would." And the two of them burst into laughter, equal parts humor and exhaustion. "Our family's been living this lifestyle for a while now. They still have a lot to learn, but they're willing. Thankfully, they aren't like most people who try and take the reins when they don't know where they're going. It takes a strong person to lead and a wise person to know when it's time to follow. I'm happy Tim and his family seem to know the difference."

There was a long pause as Emma went back to filling her sandbag and then stopped and glanced up at him. "I'm sorry, Dad. I wasn't trying to put the family in danger. After all the lights went out and the cars stopped

201

I knew it was serious, just like you'd always said. I thought if things got crazy, Brandon and his family could maybe meet us up here. I never thought they'd come on their own."

"Or tell half the neighborhood."

She shook her head.

"That's the problem with letting go of a secret," John said, scooping up some dirt and dumping it into the bag. "You never know how far it might spin out of control."

"Do you think we're safe here, Dad? I mean really safe, once and for all?"

John was about to say yes when the stillness was shattered by two shrill whistle blasts.

Chapter 41

The sounds from the whistle came streaking up the path from the road. Tim and Brandon dropped the wood they were piling and ran in that direction. John rushed to the cabin and grabbed both AR-15s and three extra magazines. When he emerged from the cabin Diane, Kay, Emma and Natalie were moving toward the gravel path. Diane had her Beretta 9mm unholstered and in the low ready position.

"Where's Gregory?" John asked.

Diane shrugged fearfully. "I thought he was with you."

"Listen, you three stay in the cabin and lock the door. If anyone you don't know approaches, shoot them."

John then hurried toward the road. Two short blasts meant a large group of individuals were moving toward the property.

There was shouting up ahead and John picked up speed. When the scene came into view his heart leapt with fear. Swallowing hard, he tried to make sense of what he was seeing.

A large group of people on foot, some of them dragging carts and small wagons, were approaching the fallen tree that blocked the path. Gregory, Brandon and Tim were on this side of the tree, telling them to turn back. For all the security work they'd done, there was only a single pistol between the three of them. If John hadn't brought the ARs they could very easily have found themselves outgunned.

The crowd wasn't listening to Tim's demands that they leave. John shouldered one of the ARs and fired the other one into the air. The crack drew everyone's attention. A second later the rifle was in the high ready position, John's finger beside the trigger guard. The next time he touched the trigger, people would be dying.

Tim spun in time to catch the AR that John tossed to him. The ragtag group frozen now on the gravel path didn't look all that dangerous. If anything, John guessed they were part of the massive horde they'd seen lumbering down the interstate a few days back.

"This is private property," John warned them. "I'm giving you all three seconds to turn around and leave before I open fire." Even though they didn't look particularly dangerous, this was a big group and in a moment like this John's charity had its limits. He'd seen plenty of selfless acts repaid by more hungry mouths when word began to spread that a veritable soup kitchen had opened up. The Applebys were the only tenants he was willing to take at the moment.

"They're gonna kill us," a little girl said.

"I won't harm anyone so long as you turn around and get off my property."

"She didn't mean you," a woman with dark stringy hair told him.

"What's she talking about then?"

The woman picked the little girl up and began walking away at a brisk pace.

"Hey," John called out after them, but they didn't turn.

He handed his AR to Gregory. "You boys keep an eye on me. If any funny business happens, start shooting and I'll cut left to avoid your fire."

Tim and Gregory nodded.

John then hopped over the fallen three and jogged down the path toward the woman.

"Miss, I can trade you some water and a tiny bit of food if you tell me what happened to your group." John wasn't just being a concerned citizen. If a group of bandits were in the area, this was something he needed to know about.

"Thank you, but please hurry, we need to find a safe place before they return."

John made a hand signal to Gregory who gave his rifle to Brandon and took off running up the path to the cabin.

"They?"

"We were in a large group heading for Oneida when we were attacked by men in pickup trucks. They stole our food and water and killed dozens. Everyone fled in a panic, running in every direction. I don't know how many survived."

"Those men who attacked you. How many were they?"

The woman blinked hard, as though reliving the horror. "I couldn't tell. More than fifteen. It all happened so fast." She started to cry and John tried to comfort her. Gregory showed up a minute later with a plastic bottle of water and half a loaf of bread. He handed it to the woman who thanked them both.

"Is there anything else you can tell me?" John asked.

She clutched the young girl to her chest. "Whenever my mind settles his horrible face is all I can see."

"Face?"

"Their leader. One side was horribly burnt." She ran quivering fingers down her cheek. "The other had the tattoo of a skull."

Chapter 42

"Are you sure it's him?" Diane asked, wringing her hands.

They were all in the cabin as John briefed everyone on the situation. The tension in the tiny space was palpable. Both families had had their own run-ins with Cain. Now it looked like he was back.

John stood before them. "I don't know of many people with skull tattoos on their faces. Plus, he was surely burned falling through the floor when the Hectors' house was on fire."

"What do you think he's doing this far from Knoxville?" Tim asked.

"I think he's come to even the score. We defeated him at Willow Creek, decimated his army and fried half his face off. Wouldn't you want revenge?"

The others didn't seem convinced. They wanted to believe Cain's appearance was nothing more than a coincidence rather than another horrifying attack.

"I don't see how he could have found us," Tim started to say before he stopped himself.

The sudden look of guilt on Emma's face was unmistakable. However Cain had found out, it had begun when she first spilled the beans.

"Look," John said. "We don't know whether that's even Cain or why he's here. If he's somehow found out about the cabin, our only choice is to finish this once and for all. Blood is going to be spilled. Each of you needs to take a moment and make sure you'll be capable of performing your duty. If not, let me know now." No one said anything. He then reached out to Emma. "Stop beating yourself up, honey. What's done is done. At this point, I need all of you sharp. Guilt at this stage will only cloud your judgment and dampen your reaction times. We were lucky today. Our security procedures were tested, which gives us time to make improvements." John turned to Gregory. "Great job alerting us to a possible threat, but staying in the area unarmed isn't good. Coming to get you at the fallen tree exposed us all to danger. Next time, sound the alarm and retreat at once back to the cabin. This is our castle keep." Then John turned to Tim. "It was brave of you to head toward the threat, but you went in armed with nothing more than a pistol. If that had been Cain and his men, he would have cut you down for sure."

Tim shook his head. "Got it."

"We also need to hand-drill more gun ports so we have three-hundred-and-sixty-degree coverage in case the cabin is surrounded."

Gregory stood up and buried his fist into the palm of his hand. "If we had a tank we could blow them all away."

The room exploded with laughter, offering them a much-needed release of tension.

"A tank would be nice," Brandon added.

Diane sipped at a cup of lukewarm coffee. "If we're making wishes, why not call in some Apache gunships?"

When they got the nervous laughter out of their system, John spoke. "We can't let these terrorists or the threat they pose keep us hiding in the cabin out of fear.

Each of us has a job to do, but we need to be vigilant and sound the alarm at the first sign of danger."

•••

For the next two hours, John and Tim used the hand drill to make additional gun ports in the northern, eastern and western walls of the cabin. They'd already made the holes in the southern wall overlooking the path yesterday and stacked sandbags around the opening.

Armed with a pistol and an AR, Gregory, Brandon, Emma and Natalie went down to the road to rebuild the camouflage protecting the turnoff that had been destroyed when the large crowd showed up. They added bushes and spread more forest debris to help hide the entrance to the cabin.

Meanwhile, Diane and Kay continued working in the garden and greenhouse, planting the vegetables and perennials.

When the last of the holes were drilled, Tim turned to John.

"I want to thank you for letting us stay here," he said. "I know we didn't know each other all that well as neighbors on Willow Creek, so you would have been justified in turfing us out. But you didn't and I wanted to let you know I appreciate that."

John gave him a half nod. He wasn't sure why exactly being thanked made him so uncomfortable. Maybe it had something to do with one of those unspoken rules he always lived by. You did what needed to be done, no thanks required. Tim wasn't cut from the same cloth, although John appreciated he was trying his best to make the present situation work as smoothly as possible.

"Space is tight, I won't lie," John said. "But having your family around has been a blessing in disguise, you might say. More hands to help around the property, and to defend it."

Tim placed the hand drill on the table. "You don't think Cain's here by chance, do you?"

John didn't mince words. "Not for a second."

Chapter 43

Just then the kids came charging into the cabin, frantic and out of breath. They were all squawking at once.

"One at a time," John said, alarmed.

Gregory worked to calm his breathing. "We were making our way back from the road when we saw five pickup trucks drive by. There were armed men in the back."

"How many?"

"Hard to say," Emma cut in. "At least twenty."

"Did they see you?"

Brandon and Gregory both shook their heads. "No, they just drove by, but it seemed like they were looking for something."

"They're searching for the turnoff," John said. He touched Gregory's shoulder. "Get Kay and your mother and tell them to come in right away."

Gregory ran off.

"The rest of you kids keep filling up those sandbags and pack them as tight as you can. Tim, take one of the ARs and keep an eye on that road. Blow your whistle if you see anyone approaching."

Kay and Diane entered just then and John filled them in on what was happening. "I'll need help from both of you with setting up these last firing positions."

Over the next few tense minutes, John pulled the kitchen table into the middle of the main room and stacked as much ammo as he could fit. From there, he placed four magazines filled with 5.56 green-tip rounds by the southern loophole for the AR. He then placed boxes of .30-06 ammo for deer rifles by the eastern and western loopholes and three other AR mags at the northern one. The shotgun loaded with double-ought buck and slugs would be kept in reserve in case anyone tried to breach the cabin door.

When they were done, everyone was on sandbag duty, except for Tim and Brandon who kept lookout.

They only managed to fill and move half the sandbags before everyone heard two short blasts from Tim's whistle.

•••

In a matter of seconds, they had all retreated to the cabin. This would be their Alamo. John just hoped the end result would turn out differently for them than it had for Davy Crockett.

The sound of the shotgun tripwire going off was the first sign that someone coming up the trail had tried to move off into the forest. Then came another blast and the screams of men in pain. More than one and John grabbed a notepad and etched two lines to mark down how many enemies were out of action.

John and Gregory took the southern loophole overlooking the gravel path. Kay and Diane took the eastern in case the attackers tried flanking the cabin. At the western loophole were Brandon and Emma while Tim and Natalie covered the south. They'd only managed to fill enough sandbags for three of the four positions.

That meant the southern loophole was relatively unprotected, except for the cabin's sixteen-inch log walls.

A voice shouted out at them from just beyond view. "I know you're in there, John."

Hearing it erased all the doubts in John's mind. It was Cain and he'd returned to settle the score.

"Your friend Bill Kelsaw was very helpful in divulging your location once we provided the proper incentives."

Cain thought he was being cute, but John couldn't help but imagine poor Bill tied up, being slowly tortured to reveal what he knew. The image, even if it wasn't real, made him all the more determined.

"I don't have a beef with anyone other than you, John," Cain shouted. "Come out and give yourself up and I'll let your family live. You've got my word on that." He paused and spat on the ground. "You also have three minutes to decide."

John turned to find everyone in the cabin looking at him, each with a different expression. Acute fear on his children's faces. Confusion and curiosity on Tim's face as he wondered whether John would comply. For a moment John wondered the same thing himself. What if Cain was telling the truth? Was a gun battle worth risking the lives of his family? What if he could trade his life for theirs? Let Cain settle the score and be done with it.

Then John spotted the stubborn scowl on Diane's face he'd seen so many times throughout their marriage.

"The rat's lying through his teeth," she growled. "And you know it."

She was right. He did.

"Cain's lied, manipulated and tried to terrorize us from the first second we met him."

"Don't do it, Dad," Gregory said tearfully.

"If I don't go out there, they'll attack us for sure," John said. "Some of you might get hurt or killed."

Tim came over and put a hand on John's shoulder. "Let the bastards try."

Chapter 44

The three minutes came and went. Finally Cain called out from somewhere beyond view. "So what's your answer, John?"

"Show yourself and find out, you coward," John shouted through the loophole.

Through the narrow opening in the cabin wall, he spotted men scurrying up the path.

John slowed his breathing, took careful aim and squeezed the trigger. The cabin exploded with deafening sound as John fired at the approaching men. Shooting a man in real life wasn't like in those fancy Hollywood movies. They didn't fly ten feet back. A man hit by a high-caliber bullet usually fell where he stood. Nothing dramatic, nothing fancy. That was what happened to the first two John hit. They dropped to the ground and stopped moving. More came up behind them, firing wildly as they made their way forward.

Rounds struck the cabin wall, the larger ones passing through and rattling a row of pans hanging in the kitchen.

John emptied his magazine, released it, popped in another and continued firing. A handful of Cain's men were circling around to John's right.

"You got a few coming your way," he called to Diane who was covering the eastern section with a deer rifle. She fired and then worked the bolt before firing again.

215

Bullets slammed through the cabin, thudding into the sandbags.

There were still men firing at them from the tree line. It appeared as though the booby-traps they'd set had taken out a few of Cain's thugs, but others pushed on and settled at the forest's edge. They were preparing to open up with AK-47s when John peppered their position. Dirt and leaves kicked in the air as rounds landed all about them. One of the men was struck through the eye and slumped forward. The other pushed himself back and out of view.

Out came another empty magazine. Behind him, Gregory was crouched low to the ground, pulling 5.56 rounds out of the box and feeding them into the empty polymer mags. This was the benefit of having four positions manned by two people each. If one was hit, there was an immediate replacement and in the meantime, the backup could keep a supply of fresh mags coming.

Course, they couldn't go on shooting indefinitely. At some point they would run out, which was why John was trying to conserve as much as he could.

"How many on your end Diane?" John called out.

"I hit three, but two others were moving too fast. Tim should see them any second."

"Got 'em," Tim replied as he opened fire.

He burned through a mag in a matter of seconds.

"Make every shot count, Tim," John shouted over the barrage. "We could be here all night."

Then John caught a terrifying sight. Two of Cain's men were in the open, lighting Molotov cocktails and preparing to throw them at the cabin. If they succeeded, it would quickly be the end of everyone inside. The place would go up like a tinder box.

John peered through his ACOG Scope and laid off three quick rounds. Except he wasn't aiming for the men, he was aiming for the Molotov cocktail. A second later, the sound of shattering glass was followed by the two men screaming as the bottle exploded and doused them in flames.

More shots continued to ring out from each of the loopholes as Cain's men tried to surround the cabin, searching for a weak point in their defenses.

John was in the process of loading a fresh mag when the sound of bullets slamming through the southern wall made him turn. Tim slumped forward. Without enough sandbags, a round had passed through the cabin wall and hit him.

Kay screamed and moved to grab hold of her husband.

"Take my rifle," Diane told her. "And keep firing."

Diane had the most medical knowledge of anyone there and it only made sense for her to be the one to assess Tim's wounds.

For her part, Natalie took hold of her father's AR and continued to return fire.

Grabbing Tim by the shirt, Diane pulled him flat on his back and out of harm's way. She then rifled through his clothes, searching for the entry wound. "Where're you hit?"

Tim shook his head. "I don't know." Soldiers with adrenaline pumping through their veins during combat often didn't know where they'd been shot.

After searching for a few seconds, Diane found the wounds. Tim had been shot twice. Once in the right arm and once in the abdomen. There were also bits of wood sticking out of his flesh that must have splintered off from the rounds punching through the cabin wall. While

217

Diane used QuikClot and dressed the wound, the others continued fighting back.

"How many are down?" John ordered. "I need each of you to report back."

"Five over here," Brandon called out from the western wall.

"Three," Kay replied in a quivering voice.

"Three for me too," Tim said quietly.

That made eleven and John had taken out seven more which brought the total to eighteen. Predictably John hadn't seen Cain show his face once during the attack. He was probably waiting to swoop in when all the heavy lifting was done so he could execute John himself.

"Emma, take over for Kay, will you." Kay wasn't doing them any good, trying to soldier on while her husband lay wounded nearby.

"Okay, Dad."

The attacks from outside began to die down. Then John spotted two men running along the tree line to his left. But they weren't heading toward him. They appeared to be running away. John took careful aim and dropped them both.

Those two made twenty and with Cain twenty-one. He was confident that most of the attackers were now either dead or gravely wounded. All except for Cain.

"I'm going outside," John said to protests from those around him.

The safe play would have been to stay inside, but allowing Cain to get away would only push the danger further down the line. Plus, not only did Cain know where they were, but he now had a good idea of their defenses. The next time around he'd be better prepared and surely do far more damage.

John rose, stuffed fresh mags into his chest rig, seated his S&W into his drop-leg holster and grabbed his AR.

"When I count to three, you open that front door," he told Kay. "Gregory, get that AR in the front loophole and cover me."

When everyone was ready, John counted to three, his AR in the low ready position. The door swung open and he moved out swiftly, scanning from left to right and moving with purpose to the tree line. That was when he saw the figure down the path by the four trucks that were parked in a line. Right away the man's mangled face told him it was Cain. Cain was alone now and trying to make his escape.

John went after him, hopping over the fallen log just as Cain jumped in the cab of the rear vehicle and backed away at full speed. Chunks of gravel sprayed as he whipped backwards onto the road, tires screeching as they touched asphalt.

John raised his AR to spray the truck, but it sped away. Making a split-second decision, he jumped behind the wheel of a '77 Dodge Ram and prepared to give chase.

Chapter 45

Cain's pickup was just ahead of him now, weaving around the occasional stalled car that blocked the road. The obstacles gave John time to close the distance between them. He came up quickly from behind, trying to decide the best way to get him off the road. A pistol appeared out the driver's side window and opened fire. Most of the shots went wide. Cain was firing blindly, trying to scare John off, but it would take more than that.

Pulling out on the left, John tried to move alongside him, but Cain swerved and cut him off. John fell back, staying on the back right bumper of Cain's truck. He then pulled to the left and dug the nose of his pickup into Cain's rear fender. It was a classic police move when trying to end a chase. When it worked well, the leading car was sent into a sharp hundred-and-eighty-degree turn. But this time, the bumpers of both trucks locked together. Cain quickly lost control and so too did John. Both trucks fishtailed violently, smashing through a farmer's fence and onto rough terrain where the vehicles flipped.

The centrifugal force tossed John out of the pickup and into soft ground where he rolled before finally coming to a stop.

The trucks continued to flip three more times.

Steam vapor rose up from the engines as John staggered to his feet. A deep gash on his head sent a thick stream of blood streaming down the right side of his face. His legs felt wobbly. His hands were shaking as though he'd just been in a fistfight with a man twice his size.

John was still wearing his Condor Tactical Vest, but his AR was nowhere in sight.

A foot kicked open the passenger door of the pickup Cain was driving. That was when the man with two faces came sliding out. The woman's description had been right on. The skull tattoo on one side of his face was largely intact while the other side was burnt and torn open in places. He now looked on the outside like the monster he was on the inside. A Desert Eagle .50 cal pistol was wedged into the front waistband of his pants.

John searched around again for his rifle before remembering the S&W in his Serpa drop-leg holster.

The two men stood looking at once another, their fingers inching toward their pistols.

"Guess it's gonna come down to who can draw faster," Cain said. "Guess that makes you the sheriff, don't it?"

"Looks that way," John said, weakening every minute from the concussion he'd suffered.

"Or we just forget all this and let bygones be bygones."

John wasn't sure if Cain was suddenly feeling his mortality or stalling for time. But he caught sight of the man's hand inching toward the pistol sticking out from his jeans.

"You draw and you die," John said.

"I thought you'd say that," Cain growled. In one quick motion, he gripped the pistol in his jeans and pulled it out, holding the gun tilted at a ninety-degree angle like the gangbangers in the movies.

Three shots rang out of Cain's .50 cal hand cannon.

John dropped, rolled and came up with his S&W, emptying the entire magazine until the slide locked.

Cain looked down in disbelief at the baggy shirt he was wearing, covered now in growing pools of blood. He sank to his knees and then fell face first, dead.

Chapter 46

Three months had passed since Cain had showed up looking for revenge. His men had been given the burial they deserved, which was to say a large pit had been dug in a clearing in the forest and what was left of them was dumped inside. Cain was left where he fell, to be picked clean by the wild animals. Nature had a way of recycling waste and it somehow seemed fitting.

Since that time, the Macks and the Applebys continued to improve the surrounding area. They had plenty of food and water and were starting to almost feel secure. Space was still an issue with everyone sleeping in the cramped confines of the tiny cabin. Once Tim had recovered from his wounds, he and John got busy cutting down trees to begin construction on the cabin that would be next door.

Their first neighbor.

Gregory and Emma had even carved wooden house numbers and nailed them in place. The Macks were number one and the Applebys number two. The next question had been a natural one: What would they call this new street? And the answer had come to all of them just as easily.

How about Willow Creek?

Thank you for reading Last Stand: Surviving
America's Collapse!

This is my first novel, so I hope you enjoyed the story.
I'm always grateful for a review. For thoughts, comments
or feedback feel free to send me an email:
williamhweberauthor@gmail.com

Want to be notified about new releases?

Find me on twitter (@Williamh_weber) where you can
join my new release mailing list.